OUT OF THE DUST OF ETERA

WRAK-WAVARA: THE AGE OF DARKNESS
BOOK FIVE

LEIGH ROBERTS

Editing by Joy Sephton http://www.justemagine.biz
Cover design by Cherie Fox http://www.cheriefox.com

Sexual events in this book are intended for adults.

ISBN: 978-1-951528-32-4 (ebook)
ISBN: 978-1-951528-33-1 (paperback)

Dedication

To all of you who have fallen in love with Etera and in wondering—

What If?

CONTENTS

CHAPTER 1

On his way back in from his rotation, one of the Akassa watchers had his sights on a figure up on the distant ridge. He was mystified as to what the krell it was doing. From the Protector's descriptions, he and the other Akassa had an idea of what the Brothers looked like, and this could only be one of them. Small, hairless things wrapped up in animal hides. He realized suddenly that the Brothers might feel about him as the Akassa had about the Protectors—frail and weak by comparison. One thing he did know; whoever it was would be in trouble if he or she lost their footing. No sooner did Byrr think that than the figure tumbled down the steep slope and disappeared into the deep snow.

Concerned and not knowing what else to do, Byrr made a mad dash over to where he thought he had seen the small person land. He didn't care about being seen as he knew that if the Brother was hurt, time might be of the essence.

The huge watcher found the body under the snow and carefully dislodged it. It looked to him to be a very young male, unconscious and bleeding in several places from cuts and scrapes presumably inflicted while tumbling down the slope. And very cold. Byrr knew he had to do something to help him, and the only thing he could think of was to take the small Brother back to Kthama.

Within moments of Byrr's arrival, Takthan'Tor and Tensil were on their way. Byrr was still holding the limp body of the young Brother, and he quickly explained what had happened.

Tensil was shocked at how tiny he was. She could see he was not nearly full-grown. "Bring him to my quarters," she said, looking at Takthan'Tor for his agreement. "We have no choice. He is in no shape to be taken back as he is, and we do not even know where they live. I will try to make him better, and then we can help him find his home. Since we are part Brother, I believe the medicines I have will work on him too."

"I agree with you, Healer. Do what you can; it is our duty to help the weak, helpless, and injured," Takthan'Tor said, quoting one of the Second Laws.

Byrr followed Tensil to her quarters, moving as

gently as he could, and laid the young male down where the Healer indicated.

Tensil covered him up with a thick pelt to get his body temperature up. She would worry about cleaning him later. She did not see any copious amounts of blood, and nothing looked twisted, so she doubted he had broken anything. Which was, in itself, miraculous.

Shortly, the Helper she was training showed up to help, and Takthan'Tor checked in later.

Tensil was confident the young male would survive. Her primary concern was when he woke up and wondered where he was and how he would react to *them*.

Back at the Brothers' village, Yutu and Pinme were frantic over where their son was. They were used to his going off on his own but not in such severe weather, and he had been away far too long. His sister, Tiva, was asking for him. They went to the Chief, who called for Sitka.

Listening to Tocho's mother, Pinme, talk about his behavior earlier in rising so early and going into the woods, the Chief surmised that Tocho had gone looking for Oh'Mah. He immediately called for a search party to start looking for him. Sitka spoke up, "He would have gone to the great oak tree. They should start there."

. . .

The Brothers looked for Tocho but found no sign of him. The quickly falling snow had covered everything. When they returned with no information, Tocho's sister broke down. Pinme stooped down and quickly pulled Tiva into her arms.

"It is my fault," little Tiva cried. "He went looking for Oh'Mah because of me. He did it for me!"

"It is not your fault," Pinme gently said to her daughter. "We must pray to the Great Spirit for his safety."

Tiva looked up from her mother's embrace. "Oh, Mama. What if Oh'Mah has him!" She then buried her face into her mother's warm neck.

"If Oh'Mah has him, then he is safe. Oh'Mah is our protector. He would never harm your brother," Sitka told Tiva.

It was getting dark. There was nothing to do but settle in for the night and do as Sitka had said. Beseech the Great Spirit for Tocho's protection.

In the Healer's Quarters at Kthama, Tensil sat quietly next to her charge. He was still unconscious, and the Healer was starting to worry about his recovery. They had piled on pelts to warm him up, and his body temperature had risen, but he still had not come to.

Darkness had fallen when the young male rolled his head to the side and moaned. Tensil looked up immediately. She spoke soothingly, knowing he couldn't understand her but hoping that her tone would alleviate his fears at being in such a strange environment. She smoothed the stray hairs away from his forehead, grateful for the dark because, if he did wake up, he would not be able to see her clearly. Hopefully, this would ease his shock at learning he was not safe at home in his village but here at the High Rocks among her people.

The rest of the night passed uneventfully. Tensil returned to her place next to him and dozed off and on. At one point, she thought of something that might make his surroundings less frightening.

As Tocho regained consciousness, the first thing he realized was that he was no longer cold; he was lying under a heavy weight of pelts. Then, as he remembered the strong arms that had lifted him, he awoke with a jolt. *Where am I? Am I home?*

He freed his arms from the blankets and lifted his head to look around. The room was quite dark, the only light coming from a line of what looked like fluorite rocks along the floor. Something told him he was not alone in the room. He slowly sat up, letting the pelts drop to his waist.

A voice spoke from the dark. He could not understand what it was saying, but he could tell it was a girl—and very young. He said hello, not expecting her to understand but wanting to acknowledge he had heard her.

More talking that he could not understand. He answered back. "My name is Tocho. Where am I? Are you Oh'Mah?"

He saw a little movement in one corner, and he could just barely make out a shape. He thought he must be imagining things because she was as tall as he was.

Then he realized there was another figure in the room. In the other corner, much taller than the first, he could make out a second female shape. There was another soothing stream of strange sounds, this time from the bigger one.

The smaller one started to come out of the corner. In the light from the rocks along the wall, he could see her feet and ankles. They were not covered in hair as he had expected. Whoever these people were, they were not Oh'Mah. But then who? He had thought for sure it was Oh'Mah who lifted him out of the snow so gently.

The figure padded across the room and then came toward him with something in her hands. He couldn't see her features very well as she was backlit from the fluorite. She made a motion that he thought was telling him to eat what she was offering him. He put his hands out, cupped together like hers. She poured what was in her hands into his. He could tell it was a good-sized serving of acorns and dried fruits. He hungrily devoured them, making what he hoped were grateful noises. After he had finished chewing and swallowing it all, she stretched out a gourd which turned out to be filled with water.

. . .

He downed it quickly. "Thank you."

More unintelligible words from her as she gently pressed his shoulder down, maybe telling him to rest. He felt her pull the covers up over him. Whoever it was, it was definitely not Oh'Mah. Exhausted, he lay back down and was soon asleep.

"That went better than I had hoped," Tensil said to the young female with her. "Thank you for your help."

"I am glad to help you, Healer. Maybe someday I will be a Healer like you," Danne answered.

"You have a kind heart. Please ask your parents for permission to return again later."

She nodded and scooted out the door.

Seeing that the young Brother was sleeping soundly, Tensil slipped out to find Takthan'Tor.

The Leader listened to Tensil's recount of what had just happened. "Your instinct to bring in a female offling was a good one. At least he has some idea now that he is not home in his village. How much do you think he could see of you and Danne?"

"It depends on how much like us they are. It is possible he could not see very much. Or, if he did, we did not frighten him, or he is very good at hiding his reaction. But I suspect the truth is he could not see very well at all."

"The test will come when daylight hits," she added. "If I can get him over the shock, I will try what I did with their Healer. Using hand signs to try to communicate."

"No doubt his people are worried sick about him," Takthan'Tor said. "We need to get him home as soon as possible, but not until he understands we mean him no harm. Perhaps this will be a chance to further establish a relationship with them."

"What was he doing up on that ridge? From Byrr's description, it was right above where the old oak tree is. Is it possible he was trying to find us?"

"I do not know how you would be able to ask him that, but it is certainly a good question."

Daylight came all too soon, and their guest would no doubt shortly awaken. Tensil fetched Danne and sent her in ahead while staying within earshot to make sure Danne was not in any danger. There was no more hiding in the shadows; this time, the young Brother would be able to see Danne clearly.

Tocho was awake but just lying there. He could tell it was daybreak from the light coming in overhead somehow. His head turned toward the sound of a rock hitting another rock. It was outside of the opening into the room. He held his breath, waiting for something to happen. And then it did.

Slowly, a figure slipped around the edge of the rock door into the room, and Tocho could not help but gasp. She had long wavy brown hair flowing over her shoulders. Her eyes were dark brown, and her skin was nearly the color of his. She had some type of hide wrapped around her, which came down over her hips, a bit like a tunic, and ended above her knees. He tried not to stare, but he could not help it. She stood still, as if waiting for him to get used to her.

She said something that he, of course, still could not understand. She made a motion to her mouth as if asking him if he were hungry again. He shook his head and then pointed to his hips and frowned. It seemed she understood that he needed to relieve himself because she disappeared around the corner then came back in with a large bowl made from a gourd, filled with soil and absorbent grasses. She set it in the corner of the room. Before she left, she pointed to it and nodded.

Tocho pulled himself together enough to give himself some relief, then returned to the sleeping mat. Within a few moments, the young female poked her head around the corner of the doorway and stepped back into the room.

She came a few steps closer to him. He could see she had a fine, downy coat over her arms and legs, which he had not noticed from a distance. They looked at each other for a few moments, then she gave a tight-lipped smile.

Tocho smiled back. The girl looked back at the doorway and said something. He turned to see a taller female, much larger than this younger one, step into the room. She was also wearing some type of covering, but it was a much lighter color. She stood for a moment just inside the door, as if giving him time to adjust to her. He felt small and frail by comparison, and he knew that due to her large size, she could seriously hurt him if she wanted to. Even the smaller one no doubt had as much strength as he did.

The female waited for his gaze to meet hers, then she pointed to her chest and said something. He thought this might be her name. So he repeated her motion and said his name. "To-cho."

She nodded and repeated it, then pointed to herself and again said, "Ten-sil." Then she pointed to the younger one and said, "Danne." She gave the same tight-lipped smile as the smaller one had.

They spent the morning together, and it seemed Tensil was a medicine woman. She showed him different objects and taught him a kind of hand language. He so badly wanted to ask her to take him home but did not know how to. Surely his family and everyone else in the village would be very concerned by now. He fretted to think of his little sister worrying about him.

After Tocho had eaten something, they left him to rest again. He didn't like to admit how much the morning had tired him out; he knew the fastest way to get home was to get better as quickly as he could. He wondered if the tall woman was the one who had been communicating with Sitka. So many questions filled his mind before he drifted off to sleep.

CHAPTER 2

Good news came to Lulnomia. Kyana announced that she was with offling and word traveled quickly through the community. Her mother was ecstatic, though her father was still estranged and sent no message back to his daughter. Eventually, the news reached Lavke.

As soon as she heard, and before seeking out Kyana to congratulate her, Tyria went looking for Lavke. She was more worried about the female's state of mind than anything else. The Healer believed Lavke had taken little note of the High Council's order to stay away from Wosot and Kyana. She seemed so overcome with jealousy and hatred that Tyria was worried the news would intensify her disturbed emotional state.

However, no one knew where Lavke might be. It was possible she was wandering around outside, trying to get control of herself. On one of the lower paths, the Healer eventually found her looking off into the distance, arms folded in front of her.

"I wish to speak with you."

"I do not wish to speak with you," Lavke snapped back, barely turning her head to acknowledge the Healer. "Or anyone else, for that matter."

"I take it you have heard that Kyana is seeded."

"Of course I have. Everyone has. You would think she was the only female ever to carry an offling."

"Look at me, Lavke," Tyria said.

Lavke did not turn around.

"I can feel the anger rolling off of you. I beg you to get control of your emotions; nothing good will come of this. Wosot moved on long ago. And so did you, apparently, at least at one time. You are with Ungut. He helped you raise Joquel. Concentrate on your relationship with him and try to let go of this bitterness and resentment."

"Stop lecturing me as if you have all the answers. What I am feeling is none of anyone's business."

"It is not until you make it other's business. If you stir up trouble again, I do not know what the High Council may do."

This time Lavke turned to face Tyria. "You do not care about me. All you care about is making up to me because I threatened to find out your secret."

Tyria had to freeze her face to keep from reacting. She kept her voice controlled. "What secret is that?"

"I do not know yet, but I will find out. There has to be some reason you left Kayerm with Straf'Tor to come to the High Rocks. Were you somehow involved with him behind his precious Ushca's back? Is the legend of the eternal love between Straf'Tor and Ushca a lie? Would not everyone be interested to learn that!"

"You do not know what you are talking about."

"Ushca was poisoned, and you were the Healer there. Perhaps you wanted her out of the way so you and Straf'Tor could be together?" Lavke sneered at the Healer, "Are you capable of that? I wonder."

Tyria was reeling inside and trying to control her reaction. "Do not be spreading any more lies, Lavke; I really worry about your future. Pray to the Great Spirit for healing from your bitterness. I urge you."

"Pfffft," Lavke scoffed. "Are you done bothering me?"

"Yes." And Tyria looked at her a moment before leaving.

Wosot and Kyana were cuddled up together. It was well past morning, but they were enjoying some private time.

Wosot rested his hand on Kyana's belly. "So, our little one will be here when the leaves start turning."

"It seems so far off," she said.

"I have not been through this before, so if I can help you in any way, please let me know."

"I will. Everyone seems so happy for us. Especially my other offling." She was speaking of Norland, Dotrat, Lai, and Somnil.

Neither of them said it, but they were both thinking, no, not everyone would be happy for them.

It didn't take long for Lavke to lose what little self-control she had. She approached Wosot outside the common eating area, just as he was about to get something to take back to Kyana.

"I heard your great news," she said. "Oh wait; are you not supposed to tell me now that I was ordered to stay away from you?"

"I am not afraid of you, Lavke. But stay away from the rest of my family."

"Speaking of the rest of your family, I thought it time you met Joquel."

Just as Wosot was about to reply, a male about his age arrived. "What is going on here?" he asked. "And who are you?" he added, staring at Wosot.

"I am Wosot of the House of 'Tar. My family and I are from Kayerm."

He turned and frowned at Lavke. "This is the male you were told to stay away from."

"I– I just wanted to—" she stammered.

"She wanted to force me to meet the offling she claims is my daughter." Wosot was not one to walk on eggshells, and this male obviously knew about the High Council meeting and the Overseer's admonishment to Lavke that she stay away from him and Kyana.

"The offling she claims is your daughter?"

"Yes, Joquel. If you know she has been warned to stay away from my family and me, you are also aware that she was spreading lies about my past. That is what this is all about. She is angry because I will not claim Joquel as my own."

The male turned back to Lavke. "What is the meaning of this?"

Lavke did not answer.

"I stake no claim on Joquel," Wosot quickly interjected.

"I should think not," the male said. "I raised Joquel; she is my daughter."

"I am glad to hear there was a male of honor who provided for her and her mother."

"Thank you. I am Ungut of the House of 'Gat. Why would I not help raise my own?"

Wosot looked at Lavke. *His own? Another lie?*

"You say Joquel is your daughter. Are you saying you seeded her?"

The male named Ungut frowned, so Wosot continued. "When we all first arrived at Lulno-mia, Lavke admonished me for not having any interest in Joquel, whom she said I seeded. I should not be surprised to find there is more to this story."

Ungut turned to the silent Lavke. "You told me it was I who seeded you. And you told this male it was him instead? So what is the truth?" His voice was rising.

"Please, not here," Lavke pleaded, looking around and noticing that others were turning their way.

Wosot said, "I will leave you two to sort it out. Do not bother me with this again, Lavke. Count your blessings that Ungut here is a male of honor. And the next time you approach me, I will alert the Overseer."

And ignoring the stares and mumblings, he continued on his way to pick up something for Kyana.

Lavke turned to Ungut. "Please, I am sorry. Joquel is yours. I just let my jealousy get the better of me."

"What is there for you to be jealous of? I do not know what to believe now–whether Joquel is mine or that male's."

"She is yours; believe me, she is."

"I am going for a long walk. Do not come looking for me." Ungut briskly walked away, leaving Lavke to shoulder alone all the attention she had brought on herself.

Wosot returned to Kyana, who was grateful for his kindness, and though she was certainly able to take care of her own needs, she knew this was his way of being tender with her. She listened as he told her what had taken place with Lavke.

"So it is over now. Joquel is not yours. And she has a male who looked after them both. He must be quite upset."

"Unfortunately, as is often the way, her lies came full circle. She set out to hurt us and ended up hurting herself instead."

"I do hope this does not get back to Joquel. It will only hurt her to know her mother has played such games. And it would be a shame if it made her doubt whether Ungut is her father or not."

Just then, there was a clack on the outside wall. Kyana's mother had come to find her. The three of them sat together and talked for a while.

"We will hope this is truly over," said Retru, "but I have to say Ungut looked very angry. As he has a right to be."

Ungut was indeed angry. But underneath the anger was the heartache of betrayal, although not because he would never know if Joquel was his or not. After his anger had subsided, he counted back and realized that Joquel had to be his. Because even if Wosot had been with her just before Straf'-Tor's followers had left the High Rocks, the timing would have been wrong. But that the female he cared for had wanted another male to believe

Joquel was his was more than Ungut could accept. That she had lied to make another male—what? Feel guilty? Ruin that male's happiness with his mate? Force him to become a part of her life? Ungut feared he would never feel the same about Lavke after this.

Pan, Guardian of Etera and Leader of the High Rocks community, was taking a leisurely stroll through Lulnomia when the Healer approached her. Tyria told Pan of her earlier conversation with Lavke and then what she heard had taken place in the eating area earlier that day. Lavke had brazenly broken the High Council's order to stay away from Wosot, so it was as Pan had feared. Now, to learn it had possibly irreparably damaged Lavke's relationship with her daughter's father only made the situation that much more dangerous. Pan needed to consult with Hatos'Mok, the Overseer.

"This is serious," said Hatos'Mok. "Not only has the female defied my order and that of the High Council, but now she has brought further trouble on her own head. Since she has so far been unable to accept responsibility for her own problems, I doubt she will take responsibility for what has happened now. Why are we so blind to our own failings, even when they become self-destructive?"

"But what do we do about this?" Pan asked. "We cannot ignore it. It will erode your authority as Overseer. Even though it was not a public proclamation for her to stop causing trouble for them, I fear it has leaked into the general community. And too many witnessed the exchange with Wosot."

"We cannot let it go unaddressed; it is true. What is an appropriate response?"

"I gave that some thought when this first happened," Pan replied. "We have no punishment other than banishment, which seems out of proportion for this situation. Or the jhorallax—even though, being so brutal, it is rarely used. But what we really want is not punishment, but to deter her from continuing to create problems."

"That is a very good point. Perhaps my order did not have an effect because there was no consequence tied to her behavior," Hatos'Mok said. "Without consequences, it seems we do not change. So, what would be an appropriate deterrent to her continuing to harass Wosot and Kyana? It has to be proportionate and just.

"Also," he continued, "what I do not understand is why we are having these problems now? In the past, there was seldom any instance of improper behavior among our people."

Hatos'Mok was right. Pan immediately thought of the rebels. First Norcab, whom her father had killed, then Ridg'Sor at Kayerm--and now there was an entire community of rebels. Could their negativity be affecting the rest of the Mothoc somehow? Affecting the very fabric of Etera?

"I agree, Overseer, this is new territory for us, and we must give it serious consideration. I suggest you and I ponder this ourselves before taking it to the High Council for discussion."

After leaving Hatos'Mok, Pan immediately sought out Irisa. She needed wisdom greater than her own about how to curtail Lavke's destructive behavior and why it might be happening now.

She also knew she had to see Wrollonan'Tor about her suspicions. Before the Age of Darkness, the Mothoc had lived in peace for eons. Was the rebels' existence somehow tied into the problems that were arising now?

Pan sought Irisa out for help with what to do about Lavke.

"You seek wisdom to appropriately address aberrant behavior. It is true, as you say, this kind of behavior is a recent problem for our people to have to deal with. In order to determine what is a proportionate response, perhaps it is a question of first understanding the motive," Irisa suggested. "Then we can address the underlying source of the problem."

. . .

"Her motive appears to be to hurt Wosot for rejecting her."

"Is it? Or is it simply the direction she has chosen in trying to achieve another objective. Seeking retribution is often the first impulse of someone who is hurt and trying to alleviate their pain. They feel as if hurting someone else will eliminate their own suffering."

"You are suggesting her motive to hurt him is really to relieve her own pain of rejection? And if she could heal the pain she feels from Wosot's rejecting her, the need to create trouble for him and Kyana would go away?"

"I believe it is possible. But she would first have to be willing to fully bear her painful internal state. To experience it, examine it. Allow it to come into the light of consciousness where it can be healed."

"Hatos'Mok, the Overseer, made a comment that we used not to have these problems. So I wonder if these problems we are now experiencing are related somehow to the negativity caused by the rebel camp led by Laborn," Pan said. "Does your father know that there is a rebel group of Mothoc?"

"He has told me of them. They are as deeply tied to the creative force of the Aezaitera as we are, so yes, I believe their negativity could contaminate the stream of the life force within Etera and ultimately affect others."

"If that is what is happening," Pan said, "then we might be faced with more bad behavior. We must find a way to address it humanely. Up until now, we have tried to protect Lavke's privacy by not revealing her bad acts to everyone. But I believe it is common knowledge, and there is even more talk now due to her recent public behavior. Perhaps the social pressure will help her control herself. But your idea of helping her heal the pain that is driving her to act this way deeply resonates within me."

"Is there anyone she trusts who could help her through that?"

"Not that I know of, but I am not close to her. Our Healer, Tyria, stood with her at the High Council hearing. Perhaps she would be the one. I will talk to her about it. If Lavke cannot control her behavior, then it will fall to the High Council to provide retribution. I wish to avoid that if possible."

"Perhaps we should seek my father's assistance. There is little he does not know, and I believe that what he is planning on teaching you next will help explain how you could go about it."

The beauty of Wrollonan'Tor's world was enthralling. He, Pan, and Irisa had walked up the stream and found a charming place to sit where he listened carefully to the Guardian's concerns.

"The desire for justice is ingrained in us all," he

said. "It is part of our need to live in an orderly world, one where there are consequences to eroding our shared quality of life. When an injustice becomes known, there will be unrest until it is addressed. But the consequence has to be perceived to be in proportion to the crime because our longing for justice expects that too."

Wrollonan'Tor stood up and stepped closer to Pan. She could feel energy radiating off of him. "Perhaps this will help you make peace with your father's choice. You wish he could simply just have left as I did instead of exiling himself into the vortex. But for his soul's peace, he needed to do just that. It was his way of trying to right the wrong he believed he committed by allowing the Brothers' seed to be used to create the Akassa and the Sassen. Moc'Tor would never have been able to forgive himself if he had not chosen as he did."

"But his punishment is out of proportion to his self-perceived crimes," Pan balked.

"Perhaps in your mind. But it was not for you to determine what consequence would be just. Your father did what he had to do, Pan. Just as you will someday."

Pan released a long breath.

"Listen to me. Moc'Tor had to exile himself into the vortex because what is coming will require all your strength to save Etera, and he knew entering the vortex himself would take some of the load off you. The evil entering the world is only going to continue to grow in strength. You asked my daughter about the rebels. Yes, the rebels are contaminating the life force coming through the vortex. As their numbers grow, their distortion will spread through the magnetic web that threads through Etera and will create more negativity.

"Much will be required of you, Pan. Your burdens may seem great now, but they will become even heavier in time. You must be the Guardian of Etera. Others look to you for leadership, guidance, inspiration. You must set the highest standards. You must have the deepest faith."

Pan was listening intently, so Wrollonan'Tor continued, "Do not despair. I will teach you what you need to know. You will receive power and abilities you never conceived possible. You will learn how to cross large distances in no time at all. In the coming age, I will send you on missions that you will not understand the reasons for. You must have faith—in the Order of Functions and in me as your guide and teacher.

"You recently desired to enter the Corridor to seek your mother's counsel. I will teach you how to enter the Corridor at will, but also how to take others with you. You will be the greatest Guardian ever to have lived."

Pan felt soothing comfort coming off of him. "How am I to learn all this?"

"Through me. Return home. Spend time with your family because soon you must leave them."

"Leave them?" Pan exclaimed.

"Remember, this is not the Corridor. Time passes here as it does on Etera. So your time here will only cost you a proportionate amount of time with them. But there will be long stretches. Seasons perhaps. This is part of the mantle of Guardianship, Pan."

Irisa took Pan's hand. "Let us go back now. I will be with you on this journey, as will my father. You are not alone; always remember that."

Pan and Irisa walked off together.

Once they were gone, a clear voice sounded in the chamber in which they had just met.

"You have done well, Wrollonan'Tor. Do not grow weary. In time your faithfulness will be rewarded."

Wrollonan'Tor recognized the voice. It was one he knew well. It was the voice of An'Kru, the Promised One. The one who, in time, Pan would teach all that Wrollonan'Tor had taught her, the sum of which, across the ages, An'Kru had taught Wrollonan'Tor himself.

CHAPTER 3

Tocho was nearly well enough to go home, and Tensil and Danne had done well in teaching him far beyond what time had allowed the Healer to teach Sitka. More than enough, and now the hard questions would come, just as they had with Sitka.

"Where am I?" he could now ask.

"You are among our people. You are safe. You are almost well enough to go home, and soon we will take you there, but we need your help," Tensil explained.

"I thought it was Oh'Mah who picked me up and carried me. But it was not; you are not Oh'Mah. Do you know of Oh'Mah?"

Tensil knew he was referring either to the Sassen or the Ancients. She was not sure that the Protectors would have been seen by the Brothers in quite a while, so it was more likely the Sassen.

"Yes, we know of Oh'Mah. Though there are other names as well," and she smiled.

Tocho had to collect himself as he almost gasped. Her unreserved smile revealed two large upper canines. Perhaps that was why the tight-lipped smiles, trying not to alarm him.

"But you are not Oh'Mah. Who are you?"

Up until now, Tensil had let only Danne see Tocho. She had not exposed him to a male, not wanting to frighten him more than he already was. Now, though, it seemed time. Having anticipated that it would come to this, she sent for Takthan'Tor.

In a few moments, he stepped through the doorway.

"This is our Leader, Takthan'Tor," signed Tensil.

Tocho's eyes widened. As large as Tensil was, Takthan'Tor was easily twice as large. Bulging muscles, a barrel chest under a thick mass of dark curly hair. And around his midsection, down his thighs, another thick full mass of hair. Tocho had never seen anything like him and struggled to control his reaction.

To Tocho's relief, the Leader remained in the doorway. "I am Takthan'Tor. I am the Leader, and this is Kthama, our home. You are welcome here."

"Was it you who left the stones for our Medicine Woman, Sitka?" he stammered.

"No, that was Tensil here. She and your Healer started communicating until Sitka was frightened by something Tensil explained."

Tocho remembered how Sitka had returned to their village so shaken up. He wanted to ask the Leader what it was, yet he was afraid to ask at the same time.

"Do you want to know what we told her?" Takthan'Tor asked the young male.

Tocho looked at Tensil as if seeking reassurance. He swallowed hard. "Yes."

"Long ago, before any of us existed, a contagion swept through the community of the Oh'Mah, killing many of their males and leaving others unable to seed offling. In order to survive, they used the Brothers' seed, and we are the result."

Tocho knew about reproduction, and his mind could not conceive how that was possible. "But how? And if this is true, how would my people not know of it?"

Tensil spoke up, "I will not explain how it was done or how it was kept a secret from your people. But what we are telling you is true. On some level, you recognized part of us as Oh'Mah; that is why you thought he was carrying you."

Takthan'Tor waited a moment for the young male to take all this in. "We mean you no harm. I want only peace between my people and yours. Will you help me?"

"How can I help you?"

"We need to take you back to your people; they must be very worried about you. I do not want to reveal us to your entire community, but I would like to meet your Leader."

"Chief Chunta."

Takthan'Tor repeated it as well as he could.

"I will help you. When can I go home?"

"We will take you in the morning. I will come to get you before first light," said Takthan'Tor. "Tensil will come with me in hopes that she can meet your Sitka again."

The night passed slowly. Tocho was unable to sleep for excitement. He was homesick, and he wanted desperately to be back with his family in the familiarity of the village. But he felt a tremendous burden to help repair the rift that had opened between them when Sitka learned how these people had come to be.

He was still awake when Takthan'Tor and Tensil entered. Tensil had brought him some food. "Eat, please, then we will go."

Tocho gobbled it down as fast as he could, then proclaimed himself ready. Looking around as he walked, he almost ran into Takthan'Tor and Tensil as they led him through the halls of Kthama. When they came to the Great Entrance with its enormous ceilings covered with huge stalactites, he had to stop and stare at the wonder of it.

When he had finished looking around, Tocho

noticed there were now two other males standing with their Leader. Takthan'Tor introduced them, saying their names. "Vor'Ran. Antham. They will come with us but stay out of sight. Are you ready?"

Tocho nodded, and they left Kthama's Great Entrance and made their way down the winding paths that lead away from Kthama.

They led him to the great oak tree by a different, less difficult route that did not require going up the steep incline he had taken in his attempt to get a wider view of the area. When they got close enough, Tocho signaled for them to stop.

"Wait here. Please. I will return with the Chief and Sitka. I do not know how long it will take as there will be a great commotion when they see I am home safely."

"We understand," said Takthan'Tor.

The morning fire was blazing, its welcome warmth shared by many assembled in the circle surrounding it. Tocho could hear the familiar chatter of voices as he came into the clearing that surrounded the village. It took a while for anyone to notice him, and then some of the women stood up and gasped, pointing in his direction.

Pinme ran to her son as fast as she could. She whisked him off his feet and hugged him voraciously.

Tocho laughed. "Mama, I cannot breathe!"

She laughed too and then set him down to look at him. She touched her son's face, smoothed his hair, took his hands and examined them, making sure he was alright.

Within moments the others caught up, and Tocho and his sister, Tiva, were surrounded by a group embrace.

"Where have you been?" Everyone seemed to be asking the same question at once.

"Safe. I have been safe. Where is Chief Chunta, please?"

The crowd parted as the Chief came over after giving everyone some time to calm down first.

"Chief Chunta, I humbly ask you and Sitka to come with me, please. It will explain where I have been. Then you can decide what to do."

The Chief raised his hand, and Sitka hurried to his side.

"Where are we going?" she asked.

"To the great oak tree," Tocho replied.

The Chief looked at Sitka.

"I am ready," she said. "I feel in my bones that it is time to face this."

The villagers followed to the edge of the clearing, where they watched as Tocho led the way into the brush and tree-line.

It took a while to tramp through the snow to the great oak tree. When they were there, Tocho asked them to wait and disappeared into the brush behind the tree. He returned in a moment with Tensil in tow.

Chief Chunta heard Sitka gasp but stood stoically without blinking.

"It is her, the female I was meeting with," Sitka said. "Ten-sil. She is their Medicine Woman."

Tensil gave her tight-lipped smile. She then turned and extended a hand behind her, and out of the brush stepped an imposing male figure.

The Chief almost didn't catch himself in time. He had never seen so large a person as was standing in front of them. The female had been large enough, but this male was enormous. Power and health radiated off of him, as did the aura of leadership. Without being introduced, the Chief knew this was the Leader of their people. It was an appropriate first contact, Chief to Chief, and it did them both honor.

They stared at each other for some time. Then Tocho looked at the Leader, who seemed to indicate that the boy should speak on their behalf.

"These are the people who took care of me," Tocho explained. "It was one of their watchers who found me. I climbed up to the peak above," he said, pointing behind him, "to get a view of the area, but I slipped and rolled down the other side. They healed my injuries. If it had not been for them, I think I would have died."

"You came to find them," Sitka said, "because I had stopped coming here?"

"I did not mean to be disrespectful or cause so much worry. I only wanted to try to make contact because Tiva was so sad when it all ended. I am sorry."

"Did they tell you who they are?" asked the Chief.

"They are descendants of the Sarnonn, Oh'Mah, and our people."

The Chief looked at Sitka as this was what she had also been told.

"What do they want?" he asked Tocho.

"They want peace between us. They are ashamed of the acts of their ancestors because what they did was wrong," Tocho explained. "That is their Chief; his name is Takthan'Tor."

Chief Chunta took a step toward the Leader, who did not move. He stepped forward again, closing the gap until he was standing only an arm's reach from the powerful male figure.

The Chief of the Brothers lifted his gaze and looked long and deep into the other Leader's eyes before speaking. "I find no dishonor in you, whatever you are. Yet I cannot reconcile myself with how you say your people came into being. I also do not understand why our Elders would have no memory of it."

Neither gaze wavered.

Eventually, Chief Chunta turned to Tocho. "You know where they live? You can find it again?"

Tocho said he thought he could. They had

watchers around, and if he could not find it exactly, he believed one of them would alert their Leader that he was in the area and would also escort him to their home.

The Brothers were familiar with gestural languages. Many gestures were used in hunting to communicate across sightlines when voices would only scare away the game.

The Chief turned back to the Leader and pointed at him, then made a circle behind him as if to tell him to go home. Then, he held his palm up in what he hoped was a universal sign to stay. The Chief then made a circle indicating himself and Sitka and Tocho and then arched it in the direction of his home.

Not knowing if the Leader could possibly understand what this meant, Tocho said sadly, "My Chief asks that you keep away from us. If we wish to make contact, we will."

Chief Chunta watched as the Leader nodded and glanced at the female. Both turned and disappeared into the brush.

Takthan'Tor and Tensil walked a while before the Leader said anything. "The female who was with them, is she the one you were communicating with?"

"Yes, Sit-ka."

"She was afraid."

"Yes," agreed Tensil. "I sensed it too."

"We must be patient. Great damage has been done by the acts of our ancestors to our chances of establishing peaceful relations with them. But, were it not for those same acts, our people would not exist."

"It seems that their males never spoke of the dreams the Ancients used to collect their seed," said Tensil. "So they have no direct knowledge of the betrayal done to them. I hope that in time we will convince them of our good will."

"No matter how long it takes, we must connect with them. It is our duty. It is the Rah-hora."

Chief Chunta, Sitka, and Tocho walked silently back to the village. Most of the people were still in the clearing, waiting for the Chief to tell them what had happened.

He held up his hand to speak, "The Elders and I will discuss what has happened. For now, do not ask Tocho any questions. What is important is that he is safe and back home. You must set this aside, no matter how difficult, until such time as I decide it is time to tell you more."

The crowd parted to let him pass, and Tocho ran to his parents and his sister while Sitka continued on to the sanctity of her shelter.

That evening, Chief Chunta called the Elders together. He told them of their neighbors and who the tall male had said they were. "For generations, our people and the Sasquatch have lived peacefully. Now I have seen with my own eyes the evidence of the betrayal Sitka told us of. Betrayal by the very ones we trusted. As for who they say they are, I believe them. I could feel the blood of the Sasquatch in their veins. It is mixed with ours but still there, so in this matter, they are our brothers."

The Chief was quiet for a moment before he continued. "The betrayal was not theirs, yet they carry the shame of it. For now, this will never be spoken of except between the Chief and the Medicine Woman."

"But what of Oh'Mah. Tocho saw two of them."

"Yes. So the Sarnonn, Nu'numic, Oh'Mah—our people have many names for them—still walk among us. Only, now, their cousins, these people, have joined us in our walk with the Great Spirit on the path of life."

CHAPTER 4

Culrat'Sar and Persica started to frequent the High Rocks, entering into long discussions with Takthan'Tor about how they might turn around their people's future. Takthan'Tor found himself looking forward more and more to the time he spent with them, and in particular, with Persica. She was bright, insightful, and very comely. He stopped fighting the idea of pairing with her, now seeing the advantages of such a match.

Persica enjoyed the time spent in Takthan'Tor's company. Though it was unspoken, she knew that her father had hoped for a match between them from the time of their first introduction.

As the months passed, the High Council members determined that they had enough requests to hold another pairing ceremony, most likely by fall. Though it would be a lot of work, Takthan'Tor looked forward to it. He was anxious to learn if the other Leaders had followed through on sending out scouts to try to find the Protectors and was hoping he would not have to wait that long to find out. He knew it was folly to think they could find the Protectors. But, perhaps discovering this was the only way those Leaders would let go of their desire to return to the past.

Kant woke up to find that Wry'Wry had again already left their quarters. It seemed she came to bed after him and left before he woke up. Now he finally admitted that she was avoiding him. Not his company as such, but any opportunity for intimacy between them. He went to look for her.

"Wry'Wry, we need to talk."

She looked up from flaking pieces off her flint stones.

Kant stopped and looked around. There was a mountain of cutting tools piling up. "What are you going to do with all these?" he asked.

"That is what you want to talk about? I am not sure yet. Perhaps I need to find something else to fill my time."

"Come. Leave your work." he coaxed her. "The winter melt and spring rains have swelled the banks of the Great River, and the sound of the passing water is soothing to the soul. The flowers are just starting to poke up through the dried grasses. It is a time of rebirth."

Wry'Wry set aside her tools. He stretched out his hand to help her up, and she took it but let go once she was on her feet. She brushed herself off and followed him down to the river bank.

The fresh air held an undercurrent of the warmth that was returning to their landscape. Light, puffy clouds dotted the blue sky. They walked quietly together for a while until Kant broke the silence.

"You are not happy here. No matter what I suggest for us to spend time together, you prefer to keep to yourself."

"It is not you, Kant. I just cannot adjust to life here. I have no memories here; there is nothing familiar."

"It will become familiar the longer you stay. Soon you will know how many steps to the entrance; you will not have to think about which turn to make at which juncture. You will know every smooth area of the walls of our space. It is just a matter of time."

"What you say is true. But it is more than that; I miss being with people I have known all my life. People with whom I have shared memories."

"Why do you not visit the High Rocks? Perhaps that is what you need."

"No. No. Thank you for offering, but I do not want to go there."

"Alright. Then why not invite your parents here? I

know your friend Tensil was here not too long ago. Perhaps a visit from them will lift your mood."

Wry'Wry thought a moment. "That is thoughtful of you. Yes. I would like to see my parents."

"I will take care of it. Now come, walk with me a while longer, and tell me about your favorite memories growing up."

Later, when Takthan'Tor received a request that Wry'Wry's parents should visit her, he wanted to ask if there was any more to the message but stopped himself. The less he knew about Wry'Wry, the better. She was part of his past now.

Before long, Tlanik and Vor'Ran arrived, and after being greeted by Adik'Tar Tar'Kahn, were taken immediately to Wry'Wry.

She ran into her mother's arms, then turned to embrace her father. "I am so glad you are here. I have missed you so," she exclaimed.

"We will be here for several days; there is much to catch up on, I am sure," her father replied.

"And we would have come sooner, but wanted to give you time to adjust. How are you doing here?" asked Tlanik.

Wry'Wry sighed. "I am doing my best, Mother, truly. But before I start off telling you about me, let me show you around and where you will be staying."

It did not take long for Wry'Wry to show her

parents around. It was a small cave system, though it did have a few branches. When they were in the room her parents would be staying in, Wry'Wry confided in them.

"Kant is kind; do not get me wrong. He is attentive, and I can tell he is really trying to help me adjust, only it is so small here. There is not much activity, and I find myself becoming bored."

"Have you made any friends?" Tlanik asked.

"One, in a way. The other toolmaker here. He showed me the best places to find materials. But it is not a deep friendship."

"Why have you not come to visit us?" her mother asked. "Or do we already know the answer?"

"You think it is because I do not want to see Takthan'Tor."

"Do you?" her mother asked.

"Yes. And no. I miss seeing him walk through Kthama's halls. I miss how confident he is and how reassuring it is to be under his leadership. But I do not miss the daily reminder that he does not care for me as I care for him." Then she added, "Cared for him. As I did care for him."

"But no longer?" Tlanik asked.

"What does it matter? No doubt he is close to asking Persica to be his First Choice." She got up from where they were sitting together and walked over to a wall, pretending to pry a small protruding piece of rock out of it.

"There has been no announcement. It is true that

the Leader of the Far High Hills is there frequently, but they are discussing community matters," said her father. "Takthan'Tor is open about his concern for our people and how a pall still hangs over us."

"It is the same here; people seem sad. But maybe that is just how people are here. I do not know."

"When can we spend some time with your mate?" asked her mother. "We would like to get to know him as we only briefly saw him at your pairing ceremony."

"We will have the evening meal together tonight, and you can talk to him all you want. He is easy to talk to, and I am sure you will like him; everyone seems to," said Wry'Wry.

"That is what everyone has always said about you, daughter," said Vor'Ran.

"I doubt that is how people see me here, I am embarrassed to say. I do not believe I am a good mate to Kant."

"She does not seem happy," Tlanik said to her mate later when they were alone. "I neither sense nor see any joy in her. She is not the same daughter we raised, but then she has not been since the end of the relationship with Takthan'Tor. Since then, Wry'Wry has been moody and irritable."

"I am anxious to get to know this Kant. Everyone spoke highly of him, and he seemed a fine fellow, but no one knows what is really happening in a relationship except the two involved," said Vor'Ran.

Kant's parents joined them at the evening meal, and the six enjoyed their time together. The two sets of parents were anxious to get to know each other, so the evening passed pleasantly. When Vor'Ran and Tlanik returned to their quarters, they could find no obvious fault in Kant or his parents, which reinforced their belief that Wry'Wry was still in love with Takthan'Tor.

"Should we talk to Takthan'Tor about this?" asked Tlanik.

"I see no reason to involve him; there is nothing he can do. Wry'wry chose this of her own free will, and it is up to her to make a life for herself here."

Tlanik wondered if that was indeed true. On reflection, she saw how she and Vor'Ran had both pushed Wry'Wry into this. With good intentions, it was true, but in hindsight, it now seemed they had been misguided in talking her into being paired.

"I think we made a mistake. We should not have hurried her into this," she said.

"Perhaps not. But it is done. There is nothing we can do but stand by her and support and encourage her to accept life here and make the best of it," Vor'Ran said.

"Maybe she will feel better when she holds her offling in her arms."

Vor'Ran's head snapped around. "Has it been long enough that she is seeded? Did she tell you?"

"Oh no. I was just imagining that having an offling of her own might get her mind off her troubles and help her move on from her life at the High Rocks."

"It has barely been long enough. But hopefully, soon."

It would take a miracle for Wry'Wry to become seeded as she still had not offered herself to Kant, though of course no one but they knew this. Kant had been above and beyond patient, but it was starting to wear on him. Not because of the waiting as much as the fear that perhaps they would never have actual relations.

"Come and sit by me," he said when Wry'Wry finally came to bed.

"You waited up for me. It is so late."

"I know. You have been coming to bed very late. And you rise before I wake. I knew if I wanted to talk to you, I would have to stay up until you came home."

"I am sorry, Kant."

"What are you sorry for?"

"For avoiding you. We both know that is what I

am doing." She sat next to him but kept her eyes averted.

"What can I do to help you?"

This time she looked at him. "You have been more than patient. And thoughtful. Any female would be blessed to be with you."

"But not this one. Not you. You do not feel blessed to be with me."

"Oh, please, must we?"

"If we do not talk, nothing will change. I cannot believe this is how you want to live your life. Or expect me to live mine," he said gently.

"I do not know what to do. I do not know how to fix this," her voice quivered.

"Perhaps if you can tell me the problem."

"I already told you, I miss my family, my friends."

Kant looked her directly in the eyes. "What does that have to do with you and me?"

"I— I—"

"I am not going to put you on the spot by demanding to know if you find me attractive. I do not think I have been unkind or inattentive."

"No, none of that. I was not patronizing you by saying any female would be blessed to be with you. You have been nothing but kind—and patient."

"Do you not have any desire for me to hold you, caress you, mount you?" he asked straight out.

"Oh, Kant. Please do not ask me that."

"Because you do not know, or because you fear the answer will hurt me?" he asked.

Her voice was beseeching. "Is there any way I can get you to drop this?"

"We can put this off a while longer, but eventually, we are going to have to face it."

"Face what?"

"Face that this is not working out for us and might never."

Wry'Wry's jaw dropped.

"You mean, you would have our pairing dissolved if I do not let you mount me?"

"It is not that, please. Give me more credit than that. But I want a partner. Someone to share my life with, raise offling together. I am not a male who just wants to relieve himself physically and then go about his own life. I want to know you and for you to know me. I want us to laugh together and cry together. Confide in each other. Share our triumphs and fears. Can you give me that, ever?"

Wry'Wry put her head down.

"I do not know."

Kant got up and started pacing.

"Then do this for me at least. When you do know —good or bad—please tell me. I will not be angry. If this is not meant to be, then it is best we both face it and move on. I will bear you no ill will, I promise. Until then, I will not bring it up again. I only ask that you be honest with me so we can move on to build a life together—or apart."

Kant headed toward the door.

Wry'Wry's parents stayed for a few days, and they updated her further about what was going on at the High Rocks. "You and Persica became friends before you left. Why not go and visit her at the Far High Hills? That would give you a break from here, and I am sure she would be thrilled to see you."

Wry'Wry thought a moment. She and Persica had become good friends and had talked about seeing each other after Wry'Wry settled in. And if she went to the Far High HIlls, she was unlikely to run into Takthan'Tor. But would seeing Persica upset her, knowing that she was probably still interested in him? In the end, Wry'Wry decided that seeing her friend was important and that she was strong enough to deal with whatever was going on between them. At least, she hoped she was.

"You know the way, though, if you wish, I will take your mother home and then return to escort you there," Vor'Ran offered.

"That would be kind, father, if you would do that."

"Fine, I will be back in a day or so. I think it will do you good to see her and get into the midst of some activity. I do understand what you are saying; this place would be too quiet for a lot of us. I suppose it is different if you were raised here."

So, Vor'Ran took Tlanik home and returned for Wry'Wry as he had said. They set off for the Far High

Hills, and he was glad to see his daughter in higher spirits.

"I am so glad to see you!" Persica embraced her friend. She then stood back, holding Wry'Wry at arms' length. "Let me look at you. Oh, you are thinner. What is going on?"

"Oh, I am just busy a lot. You should see my stockpile of tools. I have enough for everyone at the High Rocks and then some!" Wry'Wry laughed.

"I love your new wrap. Did you make this yourself?"

"Yes. That is another pastime I have picked up. I find it helps me relax."

"It is very becoming, turn around for me."

Wry'Wry did a little twirl, and they laughed together.

"I have missed you," said Persica.

"I have also missed you. Let me settle in, and then I want to hear about everything that is going on."

"Here?" Persica asked.

"Here, at the High Rocks, wherever. It feels far longer than it has been since we had time to spend together."

It was a relief to be at the Far High HIlls. It was not a tiny, cramped cave system like Kant's home. Wry'Wry enjoyed the wide expanse of the tunnels, the busy comings and goings of the people. She enjoyed hearing the offling's laughter in the background. She felt alive again, in sharp contrast to the past few months.

"It is good to be here," she told Persica and explained how quiet Kant's community was.

"You love people. I can see how that would be hard for you. What is Kant like? I have been dying to know."

"He is kind and patient, and his family is also very nice. I really have no complaints. Only that I have to stop making tools!" Wry'Wry laughed.

"You really have that many? You are a fine toolmaker. Better than I am, I have to admit!"

"That is kind of you, but I think we are equally good toolmakers. I do not know what to do with them, but I need to do something—and soon!"

"The High Council has announced they expect to hold another pairing ceremony. Why not bring them to trade? Of course, it will not be for quite a few months, but I think you should consider it."

Wry'Wry's heart jumped at the mention of the Ashwea Awhidi. "Is anyone we know being paired?" She tried to ask nonchalantly, pretending to fuss with the hem of her wrap.

"Not that I know of. But often, only those asking to be paired, their parents, and the High Council know who they are. So what do you think? It would do you good to be around the activity. And I know people at Kthama are wondering how you are doing. They would love to see you."

"Maybe. It *would* be fun." Wry'Wry changed the subject. "How about you? Are you ready to be paired?"

Persica smiled. "You know that I want to be paired; that is one of the ways you and I differed, and I cannot wait to have offling of my own. But I have not asked to be paired, no.

"So what do you do all day besides make tools and wraps?" she continued. "Have you made friends there?"

"No, not really. The females here have their minds on other things. It seems as soon as they are of age, they ask to be paired."

Persica wrapped her arms around her friend. "I just want you to be happy. Whatever it takes."

CHAPTER 5

Iria continued her studies with Useaves and had learned a great deal though there were some secrets she knew Useaves was keeping from her. She hoped to win the elderly female's trust in time to learn them before Useaves at some stage returned to the Great Spirit.

One morning when Useaves seemed to be in an approachable mood, Iria said, "I appreciate all you have taught me so far. How much more do I have to learn?"

"There is always something to learn, and sometimes there are new things we learn by trial and error. There are only a few things I have not taught you. But I will in time. I do not believe you will use them against me," Useaves said, looking Iria straight in the eye.

"Of course not. All this time, you seem to have helped me as much as you could. If you had not given me the cutting tool that afternoon, no doubt Laborn would have killed my unborn offling still within me."

"You are not long from delivering," Useaves eyed her belly. "Whose do you think it is?"

It was decision time for Iria. Either she would be honest with Useaves, or she would lie. If she lied, there was a chance Useaves would know. And even if not, Iria would know she had withheld the truth. If she truly wanted to win Useaves' trust, she had to be honest.

"I believe it is Dak'Tor's."

"Even though Laborn took you repeatedly against your will?"

"The night before I was taken to Laborn, which was a while before he first took me Without My Consent, he allowed me some private time with Dak'Tor. Based on that night and when I realized I was seeded, I believe it is Dak'Tor's."

"Well, we will know soon enough."

"Maybe. But if there are no markings like Dak'-Tor's, then we will never know," said Iria.

"If it is a male and not obviously Dak'Tor's, things will not go easy for him. The best outcome would be for it to be a daughter. Laborn will not care if that is the case."

Kaisak was hoping exactly the same thing. He would far prefer not to have to recognize it as having a right to the leadership of their community.

The community was settling down again. Enough time had passed that there was little talk of Laborn's murder or the controversy over who had apparently tried to kill him, which Useaves had revealed was Gard's doing, not Dak'Tor's. Since that revelation, Gard and Useaves had not spoken much to each other, which suited Kaisak fine. He had discovered that Gard was smarter than he had given him credit for, and now he did not have to worry about an alliance between them.

In fact, there was not much that Kaisak worried about. Useaves was training Iria. Dak'Tor and his following seemed to have quietened down. The females chosen for Dak'Tor to seed were compliant; having seen this happen before, they accepted it for what it was—their duty, with a resultant elevation in status.

The two that Kaisak had chosen to record the history of the bloodlines in the community had each come up with a different way of doing so. In the end, Kaisak assigned them to work together. Since they both had an interest in the subject and seemed to work well with each other, he felt that two like minds would be more effective than one. He anxiously awaited the completion of their investigation, knowing that allowing some of the males to mate would make him more popular. Less tortured and less complicated than Laborn, Kaisak realized there was nothing to be gained in taking Dak'Tor head-on —depending on what Dak'Tor believed about the Sassen and the Akassa. Kaisak knew he would have to find that out in time as he needed to keep the focus on the abomination of the Sassen and Akassa's existence. Then, when the time came to strike, the community members would not be distracted by internal strife.

Spring had come and gone, and the bright green of the new leaves had turned to their darker summer shade. Yellow and white summer blossoms dotted the landscape, fledglings had flown from their nests, and warmer days had arrived.

Iria sat down by the riverbed, dangling her feet in the water as she enjoyed some free time while her mother watched her son, Isan'Tor. Next to her sat her long-time friend Zisa whose life had happily returned to normal since she was no longer under Laborn's order to be seeded by Dazal.

Zisa looked at Iria's feet in the water. "Why do you do that?"

Iria smiled, "It feels good. You should try it." Then she looked off wistfully in the distance and said, "Do you ever wish you could just leave here? Go somewhere and start over?"

"I did. When Laborn told your mate to seed me—no offense," Zisa answered.

"You do not have to apologize; I felt the same way. I know you have never wanted offling, though I have no idea why."

"My entire life has been filled with strife. There was only a short period when I was younger that I felt any sense of being settled. Then, my parents left Kayerm to follow Laborn. After that, we had to leave our first home due to the cave-in. So I have had no stability. And if I have not experienced stability for myself, how could I create it for an offling?"

"So you are not ruling it out?"

"I truly do not see anything changing, so it will probably be forever. Do not feel sorry for me; I am content with my friends."

Zisa decided to try Iria's idea and gently eased her feet into the stream, making sure only to put them in ankle-deep so as not to get her lush hair wet. "Oh, this is nice. Now I know why you do it!" she laughed.

Then she became serious again. "I know you want to go somewhere else, but your parents are here, and besides, there is nowhere else to go."

Iria glanced about and then said quietly, "What about Kthama?"

"What? Where Dak'Tor is from?"

"Yes. He is the brother of the Guardian. Surely they would take us in."

"Iria, I am not a fan of Useaves, but she was right.

He was not sent to find us or spy on us; no one goes out into the unknown as unprepared as he was. You saw him. He was almost dead when they found him and you basically saved his life. I think it's obvious they drove him away."

"I do not believe that, but I am going to ask him about it. The last time I asked, he said it would be too dangerous, that we would be followed back to Kthama. If I can think of a way we can leave and not be noticed, maybe he will take my parents with us, and we can all get away from here. You could come too if you wanted!"

"I hope you find out the truth. And I want the best for you. Just do not let anyone else hear you talking like that. Your mate is apparently the solution to increasing our numbers so Kaisak can carry out his vendetta against the Akassa and the Sassen. As for me, who knows, if you did find a way to go and Dak'Tor thought we would be welcome at Kthama, maybe I would go with you."

"If I could find a way for us to escape without being followed, could we not go to Kthama and live there?"

Dak'Tor hated to see the pleading in Iria's eyes. "I know you are unhappy here. But that is not a way out for us."

"Why not? You are the Guardian's brother. Surely they would welcome you back? And now that you have a family would your sister not want to see her nephew and have us all living together?"

Dak'Tor squinted his eyes shut. It was the last thing he wanted to tell her, but he decided he could not keep the secret any longer.

"I love you, Iria, and how I wish I could take you and our family to Kthama. But I cannot. The truth is, I was banished from there and all the other communities—-or was about to be. There is no way I can go back."

"What happened? Please tell me."

Dak'Tor took her hands in his. "I am not the same person I was; please believe me. Coming here, the events here, meeting you, all this has changed me for the better. I have learned what a selfish person I was before. And I realize now how much I hurt others, people who trusted me, people whom I took for granted. And the most important one of all is my sister, Pan."

Dak'Tor told her the story of their parent's death and how he had been chosen to lead the High Rocks but did not want the responsibility. How he had tricked everyone into believing Pan was chosen by their father to lead, even though she did not want the responsibility either.

Iria quietly listened until he was done talking.

"Pan also did not want to be Leader?"

"No, but for other reasons. Our father had chosen me. He knew Pan had enough troubles to bear. It was my place to take on the leadership, and I shirked that duty. Worse, I did it without honor. I could have gone to Pan and told her the truth, and we could have approached the High Council for a solution. Or I could have grown up and accepted my role and tried to be the best Leader I could. Instead, I took a coward's way out. Worse—a liar's way out. I deserved to be banned. I only pray that in time my sister will find a way to forgive me; in my heart, I hope that before I die, she does come here with the Promised One. And only because I want a chance to redeem myself with her, a chance to look into her eyes and see only love and acceptance."

He sighed. "Not that I deserve either."

Iria scooted closer and put her hand on her mate's shoulder. "I know it was very hard to tell me all that, and I know that you mean what you say, Dak'Tor, that you regret being the person you were. And I can see that person no longer exists. I hope your wish comes true; I hope Pan does return so she can see the male you have become and realize you are so sorry for what you did."

Dak'Tor leaned over and buried his face in Iria's thick dark hair. "Thank you for forgiving me. Thank you for loving me."

They held each other for a long time.

Iria did not tell Zisa why they could not return to Kthama; she would never repeat what Dak'Tor had said, although she was relieved he had finally confided in her. Yes, disappointed that they were most likely stuck forever, but grateful he had unburdened himself. Strangely, knowing they could not leave helped her make peace with living there. This was her home and would always be her home. She vowed she would be the best mate and best mother she could and no longer dream of leaving.

The summer heat came, and it was time for Iria's offling to be born. Dak'Tor and his friends waited impatiently for news of the birth. Not being her first, she had an easier time of it. As they were standing outside the room, Kaisak and Gard walked rapidly toward the door, and Dak'Tor stepped in their way.

"Where do you think you are going?" he demanded.

"We are here to see the offling," Kaisak barked.

"The offling has not been born yet. You cannot go in there. It is for females only!"

Just then, Useaves arrived. "What is going on here?"

"Kaisak and Gard are demanding to see our offling."

"What is wrong with you? You know males are not allowed inside when a mother is giving birth. Not even Dak'Tor is allowed inside!"

"We want to make sure there are no tricks," said Gard.

Useaves laughed out loud. "Tricks? What do you think; we have another offling hidden somewhere that we are going to switch with this one?"

She turned to Kaisak, "*This* is who you take counsel from instead of me?" she scoffed, indicating Gard.

Just then, Iria's mother emerged. "It has arrived, a female. She is dark-colored like her mother, in case you were wondering."

"You are lucky it is a female because it does not matter now who seeded the offling. As for you," Kaisak leaned over and whispered to Useaves, "Lucky for you too because if it had been a male and Laborn's, you would have paid for that mistake with your life."

Iria's mother then shooed them away and took Dak'Tor in to see his daughter. Iria smiled when he came in. There was a tiny bundle in her arms, and she pulled the top of the hide back so Dak'Tor could see her little face. He smoothed the thick dark hair. "I will love and protect you forever," he said. "You are mine no matter who seeded you."

Then he stuck out his smallest finger, and the offling wrapped a little fist around it. Tears welled in Iria's eyes.

The little offling yawned, and Iria turned her around to nurse. The wrap slipped, and Dak'Tor gasped.

"What?" Iria turned her head to see what he was looking at.

Dak'Tor reached over. "Look." He pointed to a small silver-white patch of fur at the base of her spine.

Iria smiled. "So she is yours!"

"She was, regardless." Dak'Tor covered his daughter up, leaned in, and kissed his mate sweetly on the forehead. Just then, for the first time, the offling opened her eyes and looked up. Unmistakable were the silver-grey eyes of a Guardian.

"How can this be?" Iria's mother asked. "She cannot be a Guardian, can she?"

"No," Dak'Tor said. "It is just a trait, like the silver-white hair. Besides, she only has a small patch of my coloring on her back. No, she is not a Guardian."

"How can you be sure?"

"I am sure. Now please put it out of your mind."

"But how do you know?"

"She is no more a Guardian than I am," Dak'Tor said. "Trust me. Somehow I just know; my sister will be the last of Etera's Guardians."

Dak'Tor was right, to a point. His sister would be the last of the Mothoc Guardians of Etera.

As was usual in any small community, word spread quickly that Iria's offling was Dak'Tor's. Of that, there could be no doubt. Immediately chatter started up as to whether Iria had lied about Laborn taking her against her will. Speculation started that it was perhaps all a ruse to justify her killing Laborn. As much as Laborn would have enjoyed the dissent within the group, Kaisak opposed it. It did not take him long to call a meeting.

"I heard you talking about the offspring of Dak'Tor and his mate, Iria. I have been told, though I have not seen for myself, that the offling is clearly that of Dak'Tor's. Since it is a female, it matters not in the larger scheme of things. But because it has sparked an angry debate about the incident that resulted in Laborn's death, I have to address that.

"I was there directly after Laborn fell on Iria's cutting blade. I can assure you that Iria was genuinely shaken up. I can also attest that both Gard and I knew that Laborn was taking her against her will. Since he had taken her as his property, and he was the Leader, we could not interfere. Therefore, the offling being Dak'Tor's has no bearing on the female's right to defend her own life and that of her unborn offling."

Useaves then spoke up. "I had to remove Iria's son from her care so Laborn could take her. I can attest that it was against her will."

"So enough of this, then," Kaisak said. "I want no more talk of it. Let me see the female."

Iria cautiously stepped forward, her offling wrapped carefully and cradled in her arms.

"Show me what they speak of, that this female is your mates and not Laborn's?"

Iria carefully unwrapped her little head, so Kaisak could see her dark coloring.

"Hmmph."

Then she carefully held the tiny offling in front of her, letting the wrap slip down to reveal the splotch of silver-white.

"Very well. The offling is Dak'Tor's," Kaisak announced.

Iria pulled the wrap back up tight around the tiny figure.

"Show him the rest," said Dak'Tor, and he glanced at Kaisak, who narrowed his eyes.

"The rest?"

Iria caressed her daughter's tiny face until the little one opened her eyes and looked up. Kaisak caught a glimpse of the silver-grey eyes. The eyes of a Guardian.

"What is the meaning of this? Is she a Guardian?"

Murmurs broke out.

"It means nothing," said Dak'Tor. "Only that she is of the 'Tor line. You know that I have characteristics of a Guardian but am not a Guardian. It is the same with her. She is not a Guardian, believe me."

"You may be convinced of that, but I am not," said Kaisak. He motioned to Useaves to go over and look at the offling.

Iria had a fair amount of trust in Useaves now, so

she allowed the female to peer over the offling and into the silvery eyes.

"I do not believe this is a Guardian. Yes, others have displayed characteristics now and then, but she does not have the silver-white coat, for one thing. And as far as I know, that constant has never varied. Both Pan and her father, Moc'Tor, and the Guardian before him, Wrollonan'Tor, all had the full silver-white coat of the Guardian."

"Little is known about the Guardians of Etera," stated Kaisak. "For now, I will accept your opinion. But time will tell, will it not?"

He turned to the crowd. "Be on your way now; there is nothing more to see. The good news is there is another new life among us, who, in time, will help us increase our numbers so we may honor the Great Spirit by wiping the Akassa and Sassen off the face of Etera."

Dak'Tor and Iria's friends, along with her parents and Dazal and Dara's parents, hung back, waiting for the crowd to disperse and making sure no one bothered the couple and their new offling.

Dazal touched Dak'Tor on the shoulder and nodded in Visha's direction. She was standing on the other side of the crowd next to her father, Krac, and the look on her face was one of pure resentment. Dak'Tor caught a glimpse of the expression before she noticed them watching. She turned and disappeared with her father into the crowd.

"She did not look pleased," Dazal said.

"No doubt she wanted the offling to be Laborn's. There would be more glory for her if it had been and if hers has my markings. Keep an eye on her, would you?"

Dak'Tor recognized that Visha was out to cause trouble for Iria. And he wondered if it was for just that purpose that Kaisak had chosen Visha for him to seed.

At Useaves' advice, Kaisak *had* intentionally chosen Visha in order to create problems for Dak'Tor, though now he regretted it. At the time, he had thought causing strife for Dak'Tor meshed with his purposes. Now he had come to a different understanding of what best suited his goals. He was still a demanding Leader, but he saw division as working against him and not for him. However, what was done was done. Visha was seeded by Dak'Tor, and now they all had to live with the problems this might cause.

It would be several months before Visha gave birth. The community was divided as to whether it would carry Dak'Tor's markings; Iria's son and daughter did, but Vaha's by Dak'Tor did not. Now that Vaha was paired to Dazal, it seemed just as well. Easier for them to become a family without the constant reminder that Altka was seeded by another male.

After everyone had dispersed, Useaves approached the Leader.

"I will have a word with you."

Kaisak wanted to ignore her, but it was never far from his mind that she could poison him in his sleep, and no one would be the wiser. And that there had been, and would be, times when he needed something of her.

"What is it you want?"

"An apology."

"For what?"

"First of all, for not believing me when I told you Iria was seeded by Dak'Tor before Laborn violated her. Secondly, for your threat to have my life if I had been wrong. So now I want to know—"

"Know what?"

"Since you threatened me and were wrong, what is my recompense for your incorrect assumption and unfounded hostility toward me?"

"You are dreaming. You may have had Laborn's ear, but you do not have mine; I am aware of your manipulations, how you cleared Dak'Tor by turning in Gard for hitting Laborn. No doubt you only revealed that because it supported whatever you were up to at the time. For some reason, you support Dak'Tor and his family, and I have to wonder why. You have from the moment he arrived, when Laborn saw him as a threat and you convinced him that Dak'Tor was a gift."

"I see what others do not. I saw Dak'Tor's usefulness the moment I laid eyes on him. Laborn saw him only as a threat. Just as you see me that way. You are as blind as he was. You see those who can help you the most as those you need to conquer, defeat. I can be of as much use to you as I was to Laborn. Instead, you turn to that simpleton, Gard, and your insipid Krac for support."

"That is where you are wrong; Gard is not a simpleton. He has given me strategic advice, which I have followed. I trust him more than I trust you, by any means."

"Then you are the simpleton. It is a weak Leader who surrounds himself with those he can dominate so easily. You should want to be challenged. That is what keeps you sharp. Your reliance on those less than you will be your downfall. That I can promise you."

Kaisak glared at Useaves. He would not admit it but what she said had the ring of truth to it. He would never trust her, but he was still aware it was better to have some contact with her than none. Cutting her off would be the most dangerous thing he could do.

In public, Vaha and Dazal kept up appearances. They sat together at the evening fire, and in keeping with his word, he provided for her and Altka. They never argued openly; in fact, they never argued at all.

That would have required speaking to each other. Instead, they lived a separate existence while sharing Dazal's quarters. No one knew that they were estranged, not even her parents.

When they did get together in a group with their friends, she sat opposite him. For appearances, they came and left together, but other than that, they had no life together. It was how Vaha wanted it. It broke Dazal's heart that he had hurt her so. He did not blame her for not being able to forgive him, but he had loved her for so long, and it was a heavy blow.

He did not simply regret being honest with her about what he had done; he very deeply regretted it.

Altka was too young to realize that the two people she recognized as her parents did not behave like other parents. She smiled and giggled when Dazal played with her, which was often. Her eyes would widen with each new toy he made for her. When she started walking, it was toward him that she took her first steps. Dazal did not hold back with her; he loved her as his own, which she was.

CHAPTER 6

P an kept Wrollonan'Tor's words deep in her heart. She did not want to tell Rohm'Mok that she would have to spend long stretches of time away. She did not want to be away from him or their daughter that long. She started to question if she could be everything she was called to be. Mate, mother, Guardian of Etera, Leader of the High Rocks. How could she do right by all these roles? And yet she could not bear to give up any of them, except possibly Leader of the High Rocks. Her other roles were inseparable from who she was. But being the Leader of the High Rocks was a role bestowed on her. She started to wonder if perhaps someone else could serve better than she. But who?

As part of the Second Laws, the High Council had decreed that if the Leader did not produce an heir, then he or she could choose an alternative to be sanctioned by the High Council. But there was no provision if the Leader chose to step aside.

Pan thought about this long and hard. She had not been her father's choice to lead, yet her mother had told her in the Corridor that she was the best choice. Could she set aside the mantle? Was this acceptable within the Order of Functions, or would it be in opposition to what was supposed to happen? How would she know if she could do it without jeopardizing what had to happen in order to free her father?

In the end, she set it aside. She could find no clear direction within herself.

Pan spent several days in a row going back to meet with Wrollonan'Tor, but so far had not left Lulnomia for any extended time. However, she was learning to feel his pull on her, and she knew it was time to visit him again.

"In the coming years, I will send you out to complete various tasks. You will not understand the reason for them, but you must carry them out exactly as I tell you, without question."

"Can you give me an example?" she asked respectfully.

"I can, but you will not understand why, as I just said. For one thing, you will need to visit a colony of the Sassen."

"You mean the Sassen at Kayerm?"

"No. There is another group."

Pans eyes widened. "I remember a conversation about this with Hatos'Mok—that several groups of Sassen set out on their own, though they were strongly advised against it."

"Yes. They were advised against it, but they left anyway. It is one such group I will send you to, with a message for their Leader. Something very important he has to do, which is critical to the Order of Functions. He will listen to you and do as you ask without question, as you are the Guardian of Etera."

Pan felt a twinge of guilt. A stranger would do as she asked because she was the Guardian of Etera. And yet she frequently questioned Wrollonan'Tor, the Guardian of the Ages.

"The Guardian of Etera. A title it seems few have held." Pan stopped a moment then continued, "May I ask a question, please? Who was the Guardian before you?"

"I will answer your question someday, but today is not the day. Be patient, Pan. You must trust me; some knowledge has no benefit for you yet."

Pan hung her head. "I am sorry. I know I question you, and I should not. I have much to learn."

"We all do; that is part of our journey here. So, let us begin with your training."

Wrollonan'Tor led Pan down one of the tunnels to a lower level and into another long hallway, and finally into a smaller cave. The walls seemed to be made entirely of salt.

"This is beautiful. And so peaceful," she said as she looked around. "Is this natural, or did you create it?"

"This is natural. I did not create it, but I could have, and it would have had the same benefits. Do you feel more focused here?"

"Yes," Pan said, breathing deeply. "Tranquil, really."

"This is the best place for your training as the salt enhances concentration and is calming. It will also increase your energy, which is crucial for when you are manifesting the abilities I will teach you."

"The first lesson is to remember that everything you perceive as reality is made up of vibration. Everything you experience in our world, the trees, rivers, animals, clouds, other Mothoc—all exist on a specific vibratory level. But there are other levels. And on these other levels, the rules operate differently."

Barely blinking, Pan hung on his every word.

"All Mothoc pull the creative, loving force of the Aezaitera into Etera, and a Guardian more so. But as Guardians, we also have the additional ability to cleanse distortion coming from the Aezaitera that is circulating in our realm and return it to its original, positive flow. It is this power, the ability to affect the Aezaitera directly, which gives us the means also to shape it in some ways."

"Just as you are doing by creating this place where you live," Pan said.

"Exactly. Now that you understand the basis of this, you will understand what I am about to explain. I do know you wish to have your curiosity satisfied about how things work."

"Yes. I sometimes tired my father out with questions."

"I remember." Wrollonan'Tor chuckled. "And before you ask, yes, Pan, I 'died' and left the High Rocks before you were born, but I often watched you growing up. What I am going to teach you to do will explain how that was possible. Now, cloaking is a form of using the Aezaiteran flow. In its simplest form, it is just extending the vision field of an observer, so they overlook us. At a more advanced level, we actually step into a different vibration, as I explained to you when you first came here."

"When you asked me to look at that rock jutting out from the wall and change my perspective by moving and viewing it at a different angle," Pan said.

"Yes. On the vibratory level that I will teach you to create, you can travel long distances instantly. It takes no time, and you can arrive wherever you wish. You do not need to have visited the area you wish to go to. You only will it, and the creative force will take you there. In a manner of speaking, because of the Order of Functions, the place you want to go to is already waiting for you to arrive. The next level of this is to arrive while being cloaked. That takes more expertise but is essential, so you do not appear some-place and frighten anyone witnessing it. Though that too can have its uses."

"Is this why we Guardians can cloak ourselves from other Mothoc, yet they cannot?"

"Yes. Your greater connection to the Aezaitera lets you hide, even from others of our kind."

Pan's soul resonated with everything Wrollonan'Tor was telling her. This is what she was thirsty for. She could feel in her being that this was what she was called to do. To learn from him, to serve and fulfill her role as Guardian. If she failed at this, she would fail at the entire reason for her existence. So why did she still resist her destiny? She brought her thoughts back as Wrollonan'Tor started speaking again.

"Today, I am going to teach you how to travel long distances very quickly," he said.

"How far can we travel?"

"As far as we wish. The restriction is only in your mind, which you will have to fight to discipline, Pan. Your thoughts have creative power, and they will restrict your ability to do this. You must learn to stop the constant domination of thinking—to surrender, just to be. That will be the work you must do in between our visits. Practice simply being present to what is going on around you, without judgment, without trying to understand it, without internal chatter about it. Because surrendering to what is, is different than trying to understand.

Pan attempted to control her imagination, which was trying to figure out how traveling long distances instantly might be done.

"Thinking is an aspect of the Great Mind," he continued, "but it is meant to be a tool, not a master. We will practice this before you leave today."

"I am going home today?" she asked.

"Yes. Because you have not yet told your mate that you need to be gone for a long period of time. He deserves to know."

"But I have been gone for days before," she objected.

"I am not talking days, Pan. I am talking weeks. Months," said Wrollonan'Tor.

Pan could not stop a gasp. "But what of my family? Rohm'Mok, Tala? My role as Leader of the High Rocks?"

"All exist in relation to who you are. But who you are in your essence alone is your primary duty."

Pan's heart sank. "Do I not have a right to my own life? To my own happiness?"

"A Guardian's life is not their own. We are born to service. It is the second-highest calling of anyone ever to walk Etera."

"Second-highest?"

"Second only to that of the Promised One. The An'Kru."

Wrollonan'Tor knew Pan was struggling, so he gave her a minute before continuing.

"A calling is not a choice. You will have no peace

until you surrender to it. I know you have come to this place of surrender several times. And yes, I know that each time you do, more is required of you. It is not something new; we have had this conversation. There is no use in having it again."

"I tire of this battle within myself," Pan said. "I am so weary of it."

"The burden of what you are called to do is made heavier by your resistance to it. Your division within yourself, your being at odds within your own soul over who you are, these weaken you. And you need to be unified within yourself in order to fulfill your destiny."

"I need peace."

"Yes, you do. So perhaps today is not the day to explore this more deeply. If you are troubled even in this place, then you have more work to do before you are ready to begin this depth of training. Go home, Pan. Come back when you are ready. Really ready. And do not worry about how long it takes. It will take what it takes. You cannot rush it by pretending to be someplace you are truly not."

Pan tried to hide her disappointment; it seemed she had so much to learn. But, exactly as Wrollonan'Tor had just said, that was her judging herself. Learning to set aside her thoughts would be a huge stepping stone on her path.

She did as he said and returned to her family at Lulnomia.

No one knew exactly when Visha's offling was due, so it came as a surprise when she went into labor. She had been seeded longer than she had let on. Useaves tended to her while others waited outside for word of the newborn.

The birth took longer as it was her first, but in time Useaves announced that Visha had produced a son with definite Guardian markings. Dak'Tor was pleased about having another son but not pleased that the mother was Visha. He hoped her bitterness would not poison his son against him.

Visha named him Moart after her father's father.

When Kaisak learned of the offling, he called Dak'Tor to him. A concern was nagging him regarding just how many offling Dak'Tor would need to produce. His researchers had not completely finished their findings but had given him the names of several other females whom Dak'Tor could seed.

"You have another son. That makes two. Isan'Tor by Iria, and now this one by Visha. And of course, your daughter, Altka, by Vaha."

Dak'Tor thought of his daughter, Diza, by Ei'Tol, but said nothing. He wondered where they were and if they were safe.

"Thanks to the work of Jamor and Lahru, I have several more females for you to seed," Kaisak continued.

"How long will this go on?"

"As long as your continuing to seed offling does not put us back in the same situation of unsafe combinations for future generations. And as long as it suits my purposes."

"Which is to build an army with which to eliminate the Akassa and the Sassen," Dak'Tor volunteered.

Kaisak stared at Dak'Tor, remembering he did not know where Dak'Tor stood on this. After all, he had not willingly joined the rebels. This was a good opening to resolve this question.

"Do you find that thought offensive?"

"No. I have known both groups. They are not Mothoc. They are not of us," he lied. He had decided long ago that it was best he appear to support the annihilation of the Akassa and Sassen, just as those of the younger generation who were against it kept their dissenting opinions from the larger community.

Kaisak paced a bit before asking Dak'Tor his next question. "Your sister, Pan, spoke of the Promised One. What do you know of this?"

"All I know of this is that when he attains his full abilities, he will usher in the Wrak-Ashwea."

"An Age of Light? What does that mean? How do you know this?"

"I do not know what the Age of Light means. What I have told you is all I have heard my sister say about it. It was only once, and in a meeting I was attending. I never heard her speak of it again."

"When is this Promised One supposed to come?"

"No one knows. Except the Great Spirit."

"*Va.* It is I who will usher in the Age of Light when I destroy the abominations that caused us to lose the Great Spirit's favor. Who knows, perhaps it is I who am the Promised One?"

Dak'Tor did not answer, hoping that by keeping silent, the conversation would end. He did not know how strong Kaisak's seventh sense was, and he was afraid the Leader might realize he was holding back information.

"Go now. But remember the names I have given you and make arrangements to seed the maidens as quickly as possible."

"You mean for me to mount all three?"

"Well, not all together, obviously."

Dak'Tor kept from rolling his eyes. He dreaded going home to tell Iria of this. She had until now accepted his role, but this would severely test her understanding.

Kaisak had quickly reflected on what Dak'Tor told him, and once he was alone, he went to find the record-keepers, Jamor and Lahru.

"You must double your efforts to finish your investigation," he told them. "Time is of the essence, and increasing our numbers is of the utmost importance."

Dak'Tor had said that when the Promised One reached his full power, he would usher in the Age of Light. That meant there would be a time before he was powerful enough. When he would not be as strong. That would be the time to move against him. If they could find him. And Kaisak was certain that Dak'Tor would turn out to be the key to that.

In answering Kaisak about what he knew of the Promised One, Dak'Tor had chosen his words very carefully so he would not technically be lying. His father, the great Moc'Tor, had spoken of the Promised One when he told Dak'Tor about the secret crystal in the 'Tor Leader's Staff.

"It has value beyond measure. There is a prophecy that someday, the Promised One, the An'Kru, will come to save Etera. The crystal is somehow tied to him."

Dak'Tor had not yet decided whether Kaisak was an evil Leader, as Laborn had been. But either way, he realized that perhaps his time was best spent raising his offling to follow the true doctrines of the Great Spirit. If Kaisak was determined to raise an army to defeat the Akassa and Sassen, Dak'Tor would make sure that he had his own following to rise against them when the time came. Clearly, many of the rebels were convinced they were called to eliminate the Akassa and Sassen. And a calling like that was very powerful.

It was weeks before Pan told Rohm'Mok everything. Not only what Wrollonan'Tor had most recently said, but everything that had taken place during her visits with him. His ability to create his own world, what he had told of her father's need to enter the vortex, the story of the violent storm she had encountered through which she had pushed forward until she could not any longer, and the wisdom she had gained from it. Her mate stoically listened until she was finished. As usual, he was fully supportive. "Whatever you need to do, however long it takes, I will be waiting here for you. And so will your daughter."

Pan pushed back tears. What had she done to deserve this kind of love and devotion? She was reminded of the love between her father and mother and counted herself blessed among females to have found such devotion for herself.

"I may not know at any point how long I will be gone. What if you need me?"

"I always need you, Saraste'." Rohm'Mok reached over and gently caressed her cheek with the back of his fingers. "But if it comes to that, I will send Irisa."

"You must promise me that you will do so. I regret that the burden has fallen to you to raise our daughter alone so much of the time. If it is not deal-ings with the Overseer or the High Council, and now Wrollonan'Tor, something always keeps me from you both."

"Tala is still very young. You have centuries to make memories with her."

Pan leaned into her mate and tucked her head under his chin.

They rested there a moment, and then Pan sat up. "I hate to bring this up, but what is going on with Lavke? Has she caused any more trouble?"

"From what I have observed, she and her mate, Ungut, are no longer speaking much. As for the daughter, Joquel, I do not think she knows about the fight between them. If she does, she is not letting on. But with so many people talking about what Lavke did, it is sure to get back to her."

"I am not sure if Ungut will stay with her now that Bak'tah-Awhidi is allowed," Pan pointed out.

"It is a shame, really. She threw away Ungut's affection over another male who made it clear he did not want her. It was Ungut who was her companion, her provider—he raised Joquel. My prayer is that Lavke will find healing for whatever is driving her, though whether that would win Ungut back, I do not know."

"Maybe Ungut will not go as far as asking for Bak'Tah-Awhidi. We will have to wait and see."

"But," Rohm'Mok added, "at least Kyana is doing well, and I know Wosot will be vigilant and keep her close to him."

Pan let out a long sigh. "Unlike us. My love, I am afraid the time is nearing where I will need to return to Wrollonan'Tor."

This time, at Pan's request, Irisa accompanied her. She had developed a friendship with Irisa, and it was a great comfort to have someone with whom to share her troubles who had an inside understanding of them.

Wrollonan'Tor was standing in the entrance as if waiting for them. Pan knew she should no longer be surprised by anything when it came to him.

"You have been practicing presence without the intrusion of thinking."

"Yes, Adik'Tar. I am now able to quiet my mind for some time."

"I can feel it in you. You are less distracted by your past regrets and future fears. We can begin your training now."

Once again, they were in the salt chamber. Irisa had offered to stay behind, but her father asked her to join them.

"Prepare yourself, Pan," directed Wrollonan'Tor, "as if you are about to enter the Aezaiteran stream. But instead, focus all your intention on this moment; focus on your intention to surrender."

He watched Pan close her eyes. Then he said, "Ask your question, Pan. We cannot go further until you do."

Pan sighed and opened her eyes again. "What is the difference between an intention to surrender and surrendering?"

"An intention is a soul movement. It is your willingness to move toward something else. The act of surrendering is the point in time at which you bring your will into play. You cannot surrender without the will to. This is why we are working on an intention to surrender right now."

"Like sneaking up on it?"

Wrollonan'Tor chuckled. "Yes. That is a good way of putting it. We can be willing but not quite able. That is where you are now, so right now, we are working with the part of you which is willing, not working against the part of you which is not. Everything in due time. Forcing something does not work because it only creates an opposite current. We cannot work against what is; we must learn to work with it."

"Which part of me is not willing?"

"The part in which your fears live. The part that fears what will be required of you."

"How did you become so wise?"

"I know you do not mean to flatter me. I have lived for thousands upon thousands of years, Pan. Wisdom was bound to happen somewhere along the line."

This time Pan laughed. She realized again just how much she liked this Guardian of the Ages. And her heart went out to him for the eons of loneliness that he must have endured.

"You said once that you no longer immerse yourself in the Aezaiteran Stream as it will only reinforce your longevity. And that you hope the Promised One will make a way for you to return to the Spirit."

"It is my prayer that I will have served sufficiently to be reunited with the Great Spirit."

"You tell me of the heartache of your life, losing your loved ones over and over again, and your sorrow that in time Irisa will also die. Yet you would sentence me to the existence you fervently pray to be freed from? What is to become of me then? There will be no other Guardians. You have told me that yourself. So I will be the last of our kind, sentenced to living an eternity alone."

"You feel it is selfish of me to want this for myself," he answered. "Yet you do not feel it is selfish of yourself to ask me to stay for you?"

"I do not know if it is selfish. I do not know what is selfish and what is not. I do not know what is fair of me to ask for myself."

"When you figure that out, you will have your answer."

"Ohhhhh," Pan let out her frustration, causing Wrollonan'Tor to smile, but not unkindly.

"You want answers. We all do. You must search for them. Everything you need to know is knowable from within yourself."

"Oh, Guardian, riddles, riddles, riddles. What can I know to be true? What can I stand on as a solid foundation for who I am, who I am supposed to be?!"

"Discovering who we are is not a destination. It is a journey. An infinite one because we are created out of the infinite love of the One-Who-is-Three. Our nature can be no different from the One who created us. We are on a continual journey of self-discovery because we are always growing. You will never arrive at a final stagnant point, so make peace with what you know to be true of your existence at this point in time. All we can stand on is what is true within ourselves now. Because when we are in truth, we are standing in the presence of the Three-Who-Are-One."

"Are you ready now to learn how to bend distance?"

Pan closed her eyes once more and nodded. "Yes. I am ready."

"First, set your intention to surrender. And then open your mind to all possibilities."

Pan immediately recognized where she was. Kthama. She was back at Kthama, only not alone; Wrollonan'Tor was at her side. They were in the Great Chamber, which was filled with Akassa coming and going.

She looked up at Wrollonan'Tor.

"They cannot hear us or see us. We are here on a level beyond their abilities to perceive. You may speak freely."

Pan looked around the room. When she left Kthama, she had hoped never to return because all it had come to mean was loss and separation. And yet here she was. Home. Except it was home no longer. She pushed her thoughts aside and brought herself into the present. She looked at the faces, the positions, the body language. She watched the gestures, and more than anything, she reached into the room with her seventh sense to discern the mood.

"So much unhappiness here," she finally said. "Despair. Depression. What has happened?"

"The Akassa are suffering. They cannot recover from the Protectors leaving them."

"That is what they call us now? Their protectors?"

"It is not surprising, is it?"

"I failed them. After everything we have been through, all my father's plans and sacrifices, in the end, it was I who failed them by taking our kind away."

"I knew this would be upsetting. I wish I could have spared you, but you need to know the truth. They are not moving forward. Oh, a few of them are doing their best, like Takthan'Tor. But it is not enough. There is more grief than faith that they can make it on their own. Some have even gone out in search parties to try and find where our people went."

"If that is their focus, what of the Brothers? What of the Rah-hora?"

"Their obligation to the Rah-hora is forgotten by most of them. If something does not change, the future of their making will be bleak."

"You did not just bring me here to demonstrate the ability to travel distances. You brought me here because, for some reason, I need to know this."

"I could take you to the other communities, and you would experience the same thing. You need to know this because it is the truth. Because only when we are in truth, however painful, are we standing in the presence of the Three-Who-Are-One. The truth can be a double-edged blade. Sometimes it must cut in order to free us from the distortions that hold us back."

In the next moment, they were back in the salt cave with Irisa waiting patiently for their return.

"How long were we gone?" Pan asked.

"Moments," Irisa replied.

"As I said, this is not the Corridor," Wrollonan'Tor reminded Pan. "Though in time, I will teach you how to enter the Corridor at will and how to bring others there with you."

"Now that you have seen the Akassa, return to Lulnomia, Pan. But before you return to your family or any others, enter the Aezaiteran Stream and stay there as long as it takes. You need to be refreshed. This time, you may skip the Order of Functions. You need the healing power of the life force to gain balance again after our experience at Kthama. And as for blaming yourself for the unhappiness of the Akassa, you must remember that the entire High Council agreed with you. It was not your decision alone, and the Akassa's story is not written yet. They have many changes to come."

Pan went home as he told her. Irisa returned to Lulnomia, and Pan entered the Aezaiteran Stream, not realizing that it would be her longest visit there yet.

CHAPTER 7

Takthan'Tor had decided to pursue Persica. Out of respect, he approached Culrat'Sar first. The Leader of the Deep Valley was overjoyed; it was what he had hoped for. But he remembered how Takthan'Tor had looked at Wry'Wry when the two were together, and he gently cautioned the Leader not to hurt his daughter. Takthan'Tor reassured him, and with the blessing he had hoped for, decided to spend as much time with Persica as he could. The pairing ceremony was still a few months away. He wanted to be sure that this was the right choice—for them both.

Culrat'Sar said nothing to Persica but did suggest she should spend some time at the High Rocks as an opportunity to learn from another Leader on a more frequent basis. She did not question him as she was interested in matters of leadership, and she welcomed the idea of spending time with Takthan'-

Tor. She had been enamored with him ever since their first meeting at the Far High Hills–the same time as her friendship with Wry'Wry had begun.

Persica was not like Wry'Wry. Where Wry'Wry was—or had been—light-spirited and outgoing, Persica was pensive and thoughtful. She and Takthan'Tor had deep discussions about the role of the Leader and the state of the people. Takthan'Tor found her to be wise beyond her years, and the more time he spent with her, the more he was convinced she would be an asset to him in every way.

It had not gone unnoticed by Wry'Wry's mother, Tlanik, that Persica was spending a great deal of time at the High Rocks. With the Adik'Tar. She also knew that Persica had recently spent time with Wry'Wry, so used it as an opportunity to speak with her.

"I know you saw my daughter not long ago; how is she doing?"

"She has been very busy," Persica answered. "She has quite a stockpile of tools. We had a great time going through them, and I think I convinced her to come to Kthama for the Ashwea Awhidi and trade them."

"It would be wonderful to see her. I don't want to put you on the spot, but how did you find her state of mind?"

"She misses Kthama; there is no doubt about it. I

hope that in time she will adjust; she has nothing but kind things to say about Kant."

Tlanik had also found no fault in Kant, no hint of his being responsible for Wry'Wry's unhappiness. Both she and her husband had decided it must be that their daughter was still in love with Takthan'Tor. What a hopeless situation.

"Did you find her to be unhappy?"

"In some ways, yes. As I said, she is not happy in such a small community. Kant seems to have bent over backward in trying to make her happy, though. I wonder if he would consider moving here. Maybe that is what she needs."

What she needs is to get the Adik'Tar out of her heart. But what would it take for Wry'Wry to get over him?

"That, or an offling of her own."

"Perhaps!" said Persica, brightening. "I love your daughter, and I so want her to be happy."

Tlanik was conflicted. She knew her daughter was in love with Takthan'Tor. And it looked as if Takthan'Tor would eventually pair with Persica. But if she said this, it would put Persica in a terrible situation, torn between her desires for her own life and her love for her friend. And, anyway, Wry'Wry was paired to Kant, and Takthan'Tor and Persica both had a right to get on with their lives.

In the end, Tlanik said nothing, but her heart was heavy with sadness for her daughter.

Having been given Culrat'Sar's blessing, Takthan'Tor began to take even more interest in Persica. He approached her one day as she was making some tools, and they started talking. He sat down next to her so as not to interrupt her work while they chatted.

"You are a fine toolmaker. But when you are not working, what are some of your favorite pastimes?"

"Lying on the sacred ground of Etera at night and looking at the stars, how they fill the sky. Pondering the mystery of what they are. Or the firelights in late summer; how can a bug light up like that? Another mystery of our world. What an exquisite creation Etera is. It makes me marvel at the imagination of the Great Spirit."

"Yes, firelights have always been among my favorites too. If you hold one in your hand, you can watch it light up. I suppose there is a reason they do so."

"Other than just to delight us?" Persica laughed.

"Perhaps not. The gifts of the Great Spirit are plentiful, and so often, we take them for granted. What else do you like?"

"The cool waters of the Great River after the winter melt has run off. I know most of our people do not care for the water, but I love dipping my toes in the shallows. Do you know that if you do this, tiny little fish will come up and nibble on them? One of the offling told me about this, and it is delightful!

Takthan'Tor smiled. "I am not sure I would enjoy that."

"It is actually pleasant. I was scared at first, but it does not hurt; it tickles! And it makes me feel like the little fish have become my friends."

"And here I thought you had a practical mind. I did not realize your thoughts ran to fancy."

"I am not always serious. Though I am not as light-hearted and joyful as Wry'Wry."

Takthan'Tor flinched involuntarily. Hearing Wry'Wry's name with no warning, no preamble, just tossed out there had caught him off guard.

"What is wrong? Did I say something wrong?"

"No, of course not. I always enjoy our conversations no matter what the topic. Now, if you will excuse me, I need to continue my rounds."

Takthan'Tor rose to his feet and turned to leave, his jaw clenched, but he hadn't gotten more than a few steps when his rationality returned. How could he lose control like that? What would she think? He had rudely got up and walked away.

He must go back and talk to her.

So Takthan'Tor headed back. "Persica."

She looked up at him again. "I am sorry, Adik'Tar. I do not know what I said to upset you."

"Please do not address me as Adik'Tar. We have moved past that, have we not?" It was the first personal thing he had said to her.

"I think we have."

"Come with me, please." Takthan'Tor extended

his hand to help her up, so Persica set down her tools and took it.

"Where are we going?"

"Somewhere private."

Within a few moments, they were on one of the paths leading down and away from Kthama. "This is one of my favorite places," he said as he led her to a small, lush area filled with the scent of abundant summer flowers. It was along one of the shallows of the Great River—shallows just as Persica had earlier described.

"Here. Show me what you meant," he said.

"About the little fish?"

"Yes."

"Oh, do you think you are ready for this?" she teased him.

"We will see."

So Persica sat down on the edge of the little eddy and lowered her feet into the water. A smile crossed her face.

Takthan'Tor did the same, though it took him a while to get used to his feet being in the water. "I am not sure I like this."

"New experiences can be uncomfortable at first. You can do it; I believe in you."

Within a few minutes, the minnows appeared and did just as Persica had said. Takthan'Tor laughed and quickly withdrew his feet, splashing water up onto the bank.

"Seriously? That is it? You are not going to put them back in?" she laughed.

"Maybe I will. I have not decided yet."

Persica leaned forward so she could see the little fish nibbling on her toes. "I like it. As I said earlier, it is as if they are my little friends."

"I think I would like them better on a catalpa leaf, slightly warmed."

"Awhhh!" Persica gasped, then smiled. "Thankfully, they are too little to eat. Think how many it would take to make a meal."

Takthan'Tor found he really liked this side of her, but suddenly the mood turned serious.

"Was it because I mentioned Wry'Wry?"

He turned his head away; there it was again. "Yes," he finally admitted.

"Why did you not ask to pair with her if you care for her so?"

"I used to. I used to care for her. There was a time when I thought we would be paired. That was before I became the Adik'Tar."

"I believe she also cares for you. I do not understand. Why did becoming Leader of Kthama change your feelings for her?"

"My obligation to Kthama had to take precedence over my personal life. I made the only choice I could."

"Takthan'Tor," Persica said, "I feel as if you want to develop something between us, yet I am perplexed. If Wry'Wry is still in your heart—"

"Wry'Wry is paired and living her own life. It was obviously not meant to be, and you can love more than one person."

"Are you saying you love me?" she asked.

"I do." There, it was done. Takthan'Tor had grown to love Persica. Not in the way he loved Wry'Wry—had loved Wry'Wry? But it was love, just the same.

"Pair with me, Persica. Be my First Choice."

"You do not have to ask me. As Adik'Tar, you have the right simply to choose your mate. She cannot refuse."

"I know that. But I want you to come to me willingly. Not because of any authority over you."

For a long time, Persica stared into Takthan'Tor's eyes. He did not look away; he let her see into him as deeply as she wished. Now that he had spoken the truth about his feelings for Wry'Wry, there was nothing to stand between them.

"I have known for some time that Wry'Wry was in love with someone. Now I know it was you."

Persica drew her feet out of the water and rose to her feet. Takthan'Tor also stood up.

"Life is hard," she said. "I know that. I believe we do the best we can at the time. Thank you for being honest with me."

Takthan'Tor patiently waited for her to continue.

"In reality, I would not be your First Choice, but I could live with it. I think we could be a good team."

Her words broke his heart. He was not sorry he

had been honest with her, but at the same time, he was. "I wish to be honest with you. Always."

"Thank you for honoring me with the truth. I only hope in time that your feelings for me will grow enough to take the place of whatever feelings for her are lingering in your heart."

Takthan'Tor took her hand and pressed the back of it to his lips. "We will be paired then, at the next celebration."

"I will need to tell my parents."

"Your father already knows. I spoke with him before asking you."

"That was very respectful of you, thank you. Was he pleased?"

"Yes. I think it was his hope all along."

"It was," said Persica. "Before you first came to the Far High Hills, he said he wanted me to meet you. I was not prepared to be so attracted to you."

"And you are beautiful inside and out. I think it is not customary to have others know who the Leader's choice is, though our culture is new and we have not had much experience with the Second Laws. I am comfortable with only your parents knowing, if you are."

"Yes. I am fine with it."

Kyana was in labor with Pagara and Tyria in attendance. When the trouble with Lavke started, Kyana had turned to Tyria, and they had become close friends.

Wosot paced outside, accompanied by Kyana's sons and daughters and Kyana's mother, Retru. Lai, the eldest daughter, had almost finished her apprenticeship as a Healer, but chose to remain outside. It was her mother, and she was too nervous to participate.

"Push!" Pagara coached Kyana. Finally, a head appeared, and then with another hard push, the offling was born. Pagara wrapped the offling up and presented her to Kyana. "You have a daughter!"

Kyana was exhausted. It had been a long and hard labor. She took the bundle in her arms but could barely sit up to see her. Pagara finally took the offling back for fear Kyana might drop her.

Tyria rushed outside to let the others know. "Wosot, you have a daughter, and she is beautiful!"

Everyone smiled and sighed in relief, knowing this had been an arduous and taxing birth.

Wosot took Lai in with him.

"She had a difficult time," said Pagara quietly, "but everything seems to be fine. I suggest you find as many eggs for her to eat as you can, and we will see if they help. Sometimes new mothers need extra food, and for some reason, eggs seem to help."

"Is she able to nurse the offling?" asked Lai.

"I am sure she will be. Right now, she is resting. She is very worn out."

Wosot frowned at hearing this. He knew it had

been a long labor, which had concerned him. But Pagara had said both Kyana and their daughter were fine, so he tried to put it out of his mind.

"May I see her?"

"If she is not asleep, of course."

Kyana was asleep. Wosot leaned down and kissed her cheek before turning to Tyria to see his daughter. Tyria placed the offling in his arms, and Wosot cuddled her. "She looks like her mother, thank the Great Spirit."

Tyria chuckled with him. "As soon as Kyana wakes, we will let this little one nurse. Did you talk about names?"

"No; it is the mother's prerogative to name her offling. Whatever she chooses will be perfect, I am sure." Wosot leaned down and placed a kiss on his daughter's forehead before giving her back to Tyria.

As soon as Kyana awoke, she nursed her daughter. Pagara and Tyria were both very pleased when the tiny offling latched on right away. Once they were done, Tyria went out to get Retru, who was still waiting outside.

Retru gingerly approached her daughter and her granddaughter.

"Mother," Kyana whispered. "I am so glad you are here."

"So am I. How are you feeling?"

"Exhausted, for some reason. None of the other births were like this one. But Pagara and Tyria both tell me everything is alright. Does Father know?"

"No, he and I do not speak about you; he is still angry. It is his loss, Kyana. I am sorry, though, as I know it hurts you too."

"Perhaps he will come around someday. Look, is she not beautiful?" Kyana held her little one up for her mother to see.

"She is. She looks just like you did when you were born. Your mate joked that he was glad she took after you, not him."

"I love Wosot so much, Mother."

"I know. And he loves you very much as well. I am happy for you. Happy that the tragedy you went through at Kayerm turned out for the best."

Finally, Kyana's sons and other daughter came in to see their new sister. Somnil, her youngest, brought her a catalpa leaf of raw eggs.

"Ick," Kyana said.

"The Healers said you have to eat these, Mother. It will help you and the offling."

Kyana cracked the eggs open and swallowed them. They were not her favorite; something about the consistency made her want to gag. She placed the shells back on the large leaf.

"I will throw the shells out for the other creatures to eat," Somnil said.

"I am thankful I do not have to eat the shells too!"

It was a small joke, and the others laughed.

"We will let you sleep now," said Retru. "I will be back later, hopefully with some food that is more to your liking."

Kyana smiled and almost immediately fell asleep. Wosot sat down in a corner with his sleeping offling and leaned against the cool rock wall as he had done many times at Kayerm, protecting and watching over the female he loved. And now also his defenseless young daughter.

Norland announced that his mother and Wosot had a female offling. There was much happiness at the news, and it did not take long to spread through Kayerm.

Toniss and Trak were understandably overjoyed. She decided they should have a celebration for when mother and daughter were up to joining in, and she included Lai and Somnil in the planning, as well as Tyria and Pagara. It was a way for Tyria to rejoin the group at Kayerm as she had not spent much time with them since accepting their invitation to join one of their community meetings. But the warm welcome she had received then was still there, and despite the painful memories of Ridg'Sor and wanting to keep her daughter's parentage a secret, she very much enjoyed being back among them.

"This is a great idea, Toniss. We need to celebrate good events," said Norland. "Perhaps it will catch on for the births of other offling. What are you thinking of doing?"

"I thought perhaps some of the other mothers might have toys that their offling have outgrown. Perhaps we could start a voluntary, formal exchange? It would help everyone out and draw us even closer."

"I have no real opinion on that; I will bow to the females' decisions."

"The exchanges go on unofficially anyway. This is just a way to make it more of an event," Toniss said.

"I think it is a great idea. And Aerbo is due soon," Pagara announced.

Aerbo. A strikingly beautiful female with an almost pure black coat.

"We are all anxiously waiting to see if her offling takes after her or Teirac," said Toniss.

After Tyria had left Kayerm, Aerbo and Teirac had formed a relationship and paired. It would be an interesting outcome as Teirac was near as light in color as Aerbo was dark.

"Perhaps we could have a joint celebration," Tyria suggested.

The females continued with their planning, excited to share the joy of new birth in a more struc-tured manner.

As many expected it would, word finally made it back to Joquel about her parents' argument. She did not know who this other male, Wosot, was, but she was shocked to learn that her mother had tried to convince him that he was her father, not Ungut.

When she learned, she went directly to Ungut. "Why would she do this? How could she say you are not my father?"

"I am your father in every way that counts, including that I seeded you. There is no way that I am not your father. I have checked the keeping stones and know it is impossible that Wosot seeded your mother. So please put that out of your mind."

"Why would she say such a thing?"

"All I can surmise is that your mother has unresolved issues with this male. I hope she can find a way to put them to rest."

"Are you going to leave her?"

Ungut could not bring himself to tell his daughter what he was thinking. That, in the end, he might very well leave Lavke.

"I have no plans to leave her as of now. I know it would only hurt things more if I did."

Ungut reached out and pulled his daughter into his embrace. "Come here. We must pray to the Great Spirit to heal your mother's pain. Perhaps the shock of seeing this Wosot just brought up the scars of the past. Maybe time will help her heal, and she will become her old self again."

"I do not know how to act around her now. I am angry with her, father."

"We all need time for this to heal. Perhaps having

some space between you right now might be good?" he asked, looking down at her as she looked up at him.

"I could stay with my friend Shalus. Her parents have always welcomed me."

"Ask them then. I think it would be for the best right now."

Lavke came home later that evening to find Joquel gone. "Where is she? She is usually home by now." She set down the basket of longfish she had speared that afternoon.

"She is staying with Shalus's family for a few days. I think it will do us all good to let things calm down a bit. Then we can get back to normal, hopefully."

"My daughter has left our home?"

"Only for a few nights."

"How do you know? What happened? Why did she leave?" Lavke's voice was rising.

"Listen to me. It is only for a few nights. She heard that you told Wosot he was her father, and not I. You had to know it would get back to her."

"How did she hear? Did you tell her? What did you tell her? Did you blame me for this?"

"Of course I did not tell her. Why would I tell her something that would upset her and make you look bad? And no, I did not blame you. But you did do this, Lavke. It is the truth. How is that blaming you?"

"I am going to bring her home."

Ungut stepped in front of her.

"Get out of my way!" she shouted.

"Please calm down; you are making too much of this. She just needs a little space to deal with her feelings. Going after her will only make it worse."

"Worse? How bad is it? You already said she was going to be gone a few days? What are you not telling me?" Lavke lunged at Ungut, pushing him backward.

"Come over here and sit down. You are not thinking straight." Ungut tried to guide his mate to the seating stones. "There is nothing I am not telling you."

"This is all his fault. Him and his young mate."

Ungut gave her a gentle shake to get her attention. "Look at me! Is that what this is about? Jealousy? Over something that happened years ago?" He was starting to wonder just what had gone on between Wosot and Lavke. "I think it is you who is not telling me all of it. Why are you so obsessed with this male? What is he to you?"

Lavke shook off her mate's hands. "It is in the past. It does not matter," she answered, refusing to look him in the eye.

"It matters if it is causing you to act like this. I do not even know you anymore. We have had a good life together, raising our daughter. And now this."

"Our daughter had better come home as you say." She finally looked at him, only with a glare.

Ungut stood up. "I thought it was a good idea for you and her to have some space. She needs time to process her feelings. Apparently, you also do. I will come back when Joquel does. Maybe the time alone will do you some good."

Lavke got up and grabbed the basket of longfish, and threw it at Ungut as he left. She missed him, and the longfish splattered against the wall next to the doorway.

Ungut went directly to find someone in authority. He knew that technically this was Pan the Guardian, Leader of the High Rocks, but he did not feel right approaching her with this, and in any case, had not seen her around for a while. Instead, he went to her mate, Rohm'Mok. He explained what was going on and his concern for his mate's state of mind.

However, Rohm'Mok had no experience in matters like this and felt it would be best brought to the Healer's attention.

While the males were waiting for Tyria, Lavke was headed toward Shalus's family's living quarters.

The announcement stone clashed harshly against the stone wall. Shalus's mother went to see who it was.

"I demand to see Joquel immediately."

Shalus's mother moved out of the way to let her in.

Lavke stepped inside, loudly calling Joquel's name.

Her daughter appeared, a look of surprise on her face. "Mother, why are you here?"

"I came to take you home."

"I just need a few days. Go home and let me have some time alone to try to understand why you said what you did."

"You do not need your friend; you need to be with your mother." Lavke reached out and grabbed Joquel's arm, unintentionally jabbing her with her sharp nails.

"You are hurting me." Joquel pulled her arm away. A small trickle of blood was dripping down from where Lavke had grasped her.

Shalus's mother stepped forward to look at Joquel's arm. "You are bleeding. Let me get something."

Lavke pushed Shalus's mother. "Stay away from Joquel. She is my daughter, not yours!"

"Mother. Stop it. Just leave, please."

"Where am I supposed to go?"

"Go home. I will be back in a few days."

Lavke's eyes seemed to glaze over. "I am all alone. Ungut has left me. You have left me. I have no one."

Shalus's mother looked at Joquel. "Perhaps we should send for the Healer."

Lavke widened her eyes. "That traitor? The one who killed Ushca so she could be with Straf'Tor? Ha. No way would I let her touch me!"

The three females, Joquel, Shalus, and her mother, all looked at each other. They were all thinking back to the rumor that Lavke had made similar outlandish claims against the male Wosot. That to be with Kyana, he had murdered her previous mate. It seemed to add up to the fact that Lavke was in a very bad state of mind.

"Sit down, then," said Shalus's mother. "Let me make you something soothing."

Lavke reluctantly sat down and was soon holding a gourd of lavender tea.

Off in a corner, Joquel and her friend were talking quietly. "Maybe I should go home with her," said Joquel. "She seems very upset."

"But what about you? You do not need to be around her while she is like this. She hurt you."

"She did not mean to."

"No, of course not, but in this state of mind, she might do something else, unintentionally."

"I just do not think it is good for her to be alone," Joquel said, glancing over at her mother, who was sitting quietly.

"Maybe she will calm down now. Give it some time."

Tyria listened to Ungut's story.

"I could go to her, but you must know she and I are not on the best terms. She has accused me of killing Ushca to be with Straf'Tor."

Both Rohm'Mok and Ungut raised their eyebrows.

"First accusing Wosot of murdering Nox'Tor to be with Kyana, and now this," said Rohm'Mok. "How was she doing at Kthama before we left for Lulnomia?"

"Truthfully, we have never had any trouble like this. Never in all the years we were together. She never mentioned Wosot, never expressed any regrets about pairing with me. I thought we had a happy life. A good life together. I can only assume some deep-seated issue about Wosot somehow surfaced when she saw him again."

"I think it has something to do with Wosot being paired," Tyria said. "That seemed to be what brought it on. Not that he rejected her, because, at that time, he rejected all the females who wanted to pair with him. But that later, he accepted Kyana, presumably even pursued her."

"Lavke wanted to pair with Wosot?" Ungut was obviously surprised.

Tyria did not want to make it worse, so she remained silent.

"You may as well tell Ungut. He deserves to know the truth," Rohm'Mok said.

"Apparently, Lavke offered herself to Wosot over and over," Tyria reluctantly explained. "He refused her, but he also refused others. So I think that is the root of it. When she learned that Wosot did pair, it made it impossible for Lavke to believe any other reason for his rejection than that he did not want her."

"How do you know this?" Ungut asked Tyria.

"Kyana and I have become close since this all happened. We were together at Kayerm, so I have known her for a long time."

"I do not know what is hurt more. My heart, or my pride," Ungut revealed.

Tyria was sympathetic, but now she asked to be excused as she wanted to get back to Kyana and the offling. She would worry about Lavke later.

"Kyana is the one Wosot is paired with?"

"Yes. She just gave birth to a daughter who strongly favors her mother and is doing well. I wish I felt better about how Kyana is doing. She is still in my quarters for now as she is not well enough for us to move her back to Kayerm."

Rohm'Mok and Ungut both frowned but did not ask more, so Tyria hurried back to her charges.

"Are you feeling better now?" Shalus's mother asked Lavke, who looked up from the small gourd she was holding.

"Yes, thank you." She handed the gourd back to the older female. "I am going home now." Lavke stood up and looked in Joquel's direction.

"Are you coming with me?" she asked her daughter.

Joquel stood her ground. "I will be home in a few days."

"I understand," said Lavke, and she left without saying another word.

On her way home, Lavke crossed paths with Tyria, who was clearly in a hurry. "Where are you going?" Lavke shouted after her as she passed."

"Not now, please!" and Tyria kept walking.

Several other females were around, and Lavke turned to one of them. "Now, what is the great emergency that she could not stop to talk to me for a moment. Some Healer."

"Do not be hard on her. She is off to care for a female called Kyana and her offling who was born yesterday," one of the females answered.

Lavke felt as if she was standing next to herself. As if she were someone else, all of a sudden observing her own actions from a distance.

She slowly headed after Tyria but took care to stay well behind so the Healer would not notice.

Tyria came in to find Kyana in a bad state. Jhotin, her apprentice, was watching over the sick female with Pagara, who had come over from Kayerm to check on her friend.

"I am glad you are both here. Something is really wrong, and I do not know what it is.

Jhotin looked up, "Pagara and I feel we need to find a wet nurse for the offling. Kyana is not able to feed her properly."

"I know who to take her to. I will come right back." And after bundling up Kyana's daughter, Tyria hurried from the Healer's Quarters with the offling tucked warmly in her arms.

Lavke saw Tyria leave and realized that the Healer was carrying an offling. *She has my daughter. My offling with Wosot. Where is she taking her? I lost my other daughter, and now that female is taking this one away somewhere.*

She ducked into an open room and waited. Just as Tyria passed by, Lavke lashed out and struck the Healer on the head with something hard. She did not remember picking anything up, but she clearly had. Tyria seemed to collapse in slow motion, and Lavke was able to snatch the offling without much effort. For a while, she stood next to the Healer's unconscious body and cuddled the offling.

Feeling the warm bundle in her arms triggered something deep within her as if a tightly wound spring had finally broken loose. She looked down at Kyana's offling and spoke quietly. "I have you now; you are going to be safe. Wosot will be so happy I saved you from that Healer who was trying to steal you. Who knows what she would have done? She poisoned Ushca; perhaps she was going to hurt you too?"

Lavke slowly walked away, cooing to the offling in her arms. Before long, she was outside and walking up the mountain slope above Lulnomia.

Pagara waited patiently for Tyria to return. When she did not, leaving Kyana in the capable care of Jhotin, Pagara stepped outside to look for the other Healer. Suddenly Lai came rushing toward her. "Oh, thank the Great Spirit; I was going to find Jhotin. It's Tyria. Tyria is hurt. Come, quickly! She has a head injury, and she's unconscious."

Pagara hurried anxiously after Lai until they reached Tyria, who was lying prone on the rock floor.

Pagara knelt down and tried to rouse her. Tyria was breathing and still warm.

"Look, she has blood on the back of her head." Lai pointed to a small puddle barely visible under Tyria's hair.

"Did you see who did this?"

Lai shook her head. "No, I did not."

"Go and find someone, anyone, please, to help us carry her back."

Pagara leaned over Tyria again and said a prayer to the Great Spirit that her friend would recover with no damage.

The offling. A cold chill shot through Pagara. Where was the offling! She quickly stood and scrambled around the dark tunnel, feeling along the walls, not trusting what her eyes and ears told her. The offling was not there.

Was this no accident? Had someone hurt Tyria and— In a moment, Pagara knew it had to be Lavke.

"Oh no. Oh no," she said aloud into the emptiness. Then she went back to check on Tyria while she waited for help to come.

Lai soon returned with two males in tow. They gently lifted Tyria and Pagara sent Lai to find the Guardian or the Overseer. "Whoever you can find who is in authority. I will tend to Tyria, but they urgently need to know Kyana's offling is missing!"

The males carried Tyria back to her quarters, where they carefully laid her on a sleeping mat that

Jhotin, quickly assessing the situation, placed next to Kyana.

Pagara then examined Tyria more closely. She tried to calm her mind, which was racing with worry about Kyana's offling, and she told Jhotin what she thought must have happened.

Lai hurried as quickly as she could through the halls of Lulnomia, her heart cold with worry for her missing newborn sister. On her way, she came across Pan's sisters, Vel and Inrion, who were talking together.

"Oh, please! Do you know where Pan is? Or the Overseer? Anyone? Something terrible has happened."

"No, but we just went to ask Rohm'Mok a question, and he is with Ungut. What happened?"

"Someone hit the Healer, Tyria, over the head. And my mother's new offling—my sister—is missing. We think it might have been Lavke."

The three females took off and burst into the room where Rohm'Mok and Lavke's mate were still talking.

"Where would Lavke have taken the offling?" Rohm'Mok asked Ungut after hearing what had happened.

"I have no idea. Certainly not home. That is the first place anyone would look."

"Then we have to assume she has taken her outside. They could be anywhere," Rohm'Mok said.

"The offling needs to nurse; she cannot be kept away for that long. Tyria was taking her to a wet nurse when she was attacked."

"Is your mother not able to nurse her daughter?"

"Yes. No. She was, but she is not well and is not producing enough milk," Lai explained. "The offling needs more than she can provide."

Rohm'Mok nodded. "We need to find the Overseer immediately."

Somehow, news of Kyana's missing offling had made its way to members of both the Kayerm and the High Rocks communities. A crowd of Mothoc was bustling with concern, and there was flustered talk of organizing search parties.

Hatos'Mok raised his hands for quiet. "Please, you must remain calm. We do not know that the female Lavke has taken the offling of Wosot and Kyana of Kayerm, but at this point, we have to assume it is so. No one has seen Lavke since the Healer was attacked, though we do know she had just left the place where her daughter, Joquel, is staying."

"She seemed fine when she left us!" Joquel called out.

She turned to her father and whispered, "Surely Mother will not hurt the offling?"

Ungut did not know what to say. The Lavke he knew would never hurt an offling, but he could not be certain of whoever she had turned into.

"I need everyone to stay inside Lulnomia," Hatos'Mok continued. "It is important that Lavke not feel attacked or surrounded, so you all need to stay away. I know you want to help, but this is a fragile situation, and we have to move carefully."

"Where is Pan?" someone shouted. "Where is the Guardian?"

Rohm'Mok did not want to say that Pan was away learning from an ancient Guardian they all believed had died centuries before, but Kyana's mate rescued him.

"You cannot expect me to stay here and do nothing?" Wosot was uncharacteristically beside himself.

"That is exactly what I expect you to do," said the Overseer. "You are the last person she needs to see. We know it was her jealousy of you and Kyana that set this off— This— Whatever it is that is happening to Lavke."

"No one has any idea where she could be?" asked Lai.

Unnoticed by everyone, a peculiar look came over Joquel. In a flash, she knew where her mother had taken Kyana's daughter.

The Overseer dismissed everyone, again admonishing them not to get involved.

Ungut turned to his daughter, "Where will you be?"

"I think I should come home and be with you. I will see you a little later, though, if that is alright?"

Ungut hugged her. "I will be waiting for you. We must pray to the Great Spirit for intervention."

Joquel acted as if she was looking for her friend, Shalus, and hovered around the Great Entrance while the crowd dispersed. After her father was clearly out of sight and no one seemed to be watching, she slipped out of Lulnomia.

The offling in Lavke's arms had started crying. She sat rocking the bundle. "There, there. Mother is here. Shhhhh."

It was a beautiful setting with lush green grasses underfoot at the base of a large fir, its soft boughs providing a cozy canopy. The warm autumn sun breaking through the openings in the branches was warm on Lavke's shoulders.

Lavke felt at peace. She finally had what she had wanted for so long. Wosot's daughter, her daughter—their daughter—was finally cradled safely in her arms. Her life would soon begin anew. She had waited so long for this moment, and now it was here.

Her reverie was broken by the sound of someone coming up the path. She looked up, seeing a figure she did not recognize.

"Mother," the figure said.

Lavke didn't answer, and the female repeated it, "Mother. What are you doing?" Then the female glanced downward to the fussing offling.

"Who are you? Do I know you?"

"I'm Joquel. Your daughter."

"You are not Joquel. You are not my daughter. This is my daughter, Joquel," Lavke looked down at the offling.

"Mother, I need you to come home with me."

"I do not know who you are, but I am not your mother. Please go away. My mate will be here any minute to take us home."

The female just stood there, and Lavke did not really know what to do.

"She looks newborn. May I see her?" The female took a step forward. Lavke looked her up and down. Something did seem remotely familiar. Lavke decided she could at least let her look at the offling. "Yes, you can come closer."

Lavke kept her eye on the female who had said her name was Joquel. She moved slowly, which made Lavke feel a little better.

"She is beautiful."

"Thank you. I named her after my mother."

For some reason, that seemed to affect this other Joquel, as her eyes teared up.

"Are you sure you do not want help? I can help you get down the path. It must not have been easy getting up here carrying her."

"It was not, that is true. But I am not ready to leave yet. As I said, I am waiting for my mate."

"Do you want me to go get him for you? I think I know who he is. Maybe he is lost on the path?"

Lavke thought a moment. For some reason, she couldn't remember Wosot ever being up here with her, though she could have sworn that this was one of their favorite spots. They had found it when they first came here. But where was here? Suddenly Lavke was confused. Perhaps she did need this young female's help.

"Maybe you could go and see if he is lost. Are you sure you know which one he is?"

"Oh yes. Absolutely. I have seen you with him before, I believe."

Lavke was having a hard time thinking. "Yes, I am sure you have. Thank you."

"Wait here. I will be right back!"

Lavke sat there with her newborn daughter for what seemed like a long time. Finally, she saw motion out of the corner of her eye and saw the other Joquel coming up the path. And she had Wosot with her.

Lavke's heart leaped! It was her beloved. She tried to get up to go and embrace him, but she couldn't quite rise with the way she was holding Joquel.

"Do not get up. I will come to you," Wosot said.

Lavke waited patiently for Wosot. He crouched in front of her and glanced down at their daughter.

"She is very fussy. I think she needs her nap," Lavke said.

"Well, then, let me help you get her home. Here, let me take her from you so you can get down safely."

Lavke handed over Joquel. Then her head started hurting. "Oh. Something is wrong. I feel peculiar."

"Are you dizzy, Mother— Lavke? Let me help you up."

Lavke got to her feet with help from the young female who called herself Joquel and leaned on her arm as they made it down the path. "Where are we going?" she asked.

"Home. You said you wanted to go home."

They made it carefully down the path to where there was another male waiting for them.

"Who is that?"

"He is here to help you," the other Joquel answered, still holding onto Lavke's arm.

"Does he know I am dizzy?" Lavke asked.

"No, but he has something for you to drink that will make you feel better all round!"

Suddenly Lavke panicked. "Where is Wosot? Where is Joquel?" She looked around frantically.

"They are right there. See? A bit past this male. They just traveled a little faster than we did."

Wosot waved at her, and she could see him.

Then the older Joquel took a gourd from the male who wasn't Wosot and handed it to Lavke. "Please drink this. It will help. I promise. We will make sure your daughter gets her nap. Let me take care of you right now."

Lavke squinted at this other male, whose face was difficult to see against the eastern sunlight. "I— I — I think I might know you."

"Do not worry about that right now. You need to rest, alright?"

The male's voice was suddenly very comforting to Lavke, and she let them lead her into a beautiful cave the likes of which she had never seen before. "It is so tranquil here."

"Yes, it is. Come."

Soon Lavke was resting on a very soft mat in a comfortable room with shafts of sunlight coming in overhead. She felt drowsy. Before she drifted off, she noticed that the female was still with her, so slowly, she reached out her hand.

"Joquel?" she struggled to say.

"Yes, Mother, I am right here. Rest now, Mother."

Lavke let herself drift off to sleep, Joquel's hand in hers letting her know that she was not alone.

Lai had met Wosot on the mountain, and together they rushed the offling to Tyria's quarters. By the time they arrived, Pagara had treated Tyria's head wound, and she was conscious but a little disoriented.

After Pagara and Lai had checked her over,

Wosot whisked his daughter to the wet nurse who had been waiting there for a while, and the offling stopped crying the moment she started to nurse.

Then Wosot turned to his mate, lying so motionless on the sleeping mat. She hadn't even reacted to her offling's frantic, hungry cries. "Pagara, tell me she is going to get better?"

"Something is really wrong, and I do not know what. She is fading fast," said Pagara, deep concern in her voice.

"Irisa. Oh my goodness, Irisa," Tyria said weakly, trying to prop herself up on one elbow. "Why did I not think of her sooner? Please, send someone to find Irisa. Send everyone you can to find her! Tell her how Kyana is."

It felt like forever before Lai returned with Irisa. The older female had something in her hands, something wrapped in a soft hide, and she stepped across the room and knelt down by Kyana. She put two fingers into the package before placing them in Kyana's mouth. Then she did it again. After a few moments, Kyana rolled her head to the side and moaned.

Wosot nearly broke down with relief. "Whatever you are doing, it is helping!"

Irisa continued ministering to Kyana and then sat patiently waiting. Within a few hours, Kyana had come around and was sitting up and drinking water.

Wosot could not help himself; he hugged Irisa

tightly, though gently. His face was lit up by a huge grin.

"What did you give her? What was wrong with her?" Pagara asked.

"I gave her honey. I have seen this before, after a long and hard birth. I imagine she has not eaten for some time?"

"Yes. We gave her eggs, and they did not help. But the honey did," Lai added. She was smiling broadly.

"Anything sweet seems to work, fruit, nectar. But honey is the best because it seems to act the quickest, and it keeps without spoiling."

"Do we need to continue giving it to her?" asked Lai.

"She needs to eat a balanced meal as soon as she is willing, but until then, yes, you must let her have some—and make sure it is regularly."

"How did you know what to do?" asked Wosot, now seated next to Kyana, his hands folded around hers.

"The moment Lai told me how Kyana was acting, I knew what it was."

"Thank you, Lai," Wosot said, now very grave. "Thank you, Tyria. Kyana owes you both her life."

"It was not her time," said Irisa.

"How do you know?" Lai asked.

"Because she did not die."

No one said a word; they were too tired to entertain such deep thoughts.

"I believe there is more to the story than just Kyana going downhill after giving birth," Irisa said.

Together, the others in the room pieced together the story of Lavke's obsession with Wosot and Kyana and the events of the morning, including Lavke's apparent break with reality.

"Where is this Lavke now?" Irisa asked.

"She is in Pagara's Healer's Quarters with Jhotin. We were afraid to take her home to her mate," Tyria explained. "We were afraid seeing him might make her delusion worse, and Jhotin couldn't bring her here."

Pagara had been thrilled to see Irisa. As the two made their way to Pagara's quarters to check on Lavke, she told Irisa every bit of what she knew about Lavke's condition.

She added, "Apparently, Lavke did seem to recognize her daughter just before dozing off."

"The mind is an amazing creation. Sometimes it bends reality to protect us from a pain we cannot bear to face. In this instance, I believe it was Kyana having the offling that Lavke had wanted so badly. I am not sure if her pairing with Ungut will survive this, but there is a chance she may come out of it and be alright."

"Alright? As in forever?" asked Pagara.

"Yes. In her mind, she achieved that which she

wanted so much. So much so that she lied about who Joquel's father was. In the make-believe world she had entered, it was finally true. She had the offling that she believed was hers and Wosot's. Perhaps now she will be able to let go of it and heal."

They stepped quietly inside. Joquel was still sitting there, holding her mother's hand.

After greeting them both and nodding to Joquel, Jhotin slipped out, his work now done.

Irisa walked over and sat next to Lavke and her daughter.

"People say you are special," Joquel said. "That you know things others do not. That you see what others do not. Please tell me my mother is going to recover." The pleading in her eyes matched that in her words.

Irisa leaned over and placed one wizened hand on Lavke's forehead and the other over Lavke's heart and closed her eyes. Lavke seemed to relax even more under her touch.

A stillness came over the room and the four females in it, almost as if a warm, soothing breeze was passing over them all. And they felt a peace they had not ever experienced before. It lasted until Irisa removed her hands.

She looked at Pagara, then at Joquel, and simply smiled and nodded. Then slowly, she got up and left.

Both Pagara and Joquel knew they had witnessed a sacred moment. They never spoke of it to anyone, nor did they question Irisa about it. They had heard the miraculous stories of the old female's healing abilities. This one would remain their own private memory.

Lavke awoke the next day. She looked around and saw Pagara. "Where am I? Who are you?"

Pagara came to her side. "I am the Healer at Kayerm, and you are in my Healer's Quarters. Here, sit up and drink this."

"How long have I been here?"

"Just since yesterday. About a day."

Lavke gulped it down. "Ah. I was so thirsty, thank you."

Pagara brought her some more water.

"I did something terrible. Yes?"

"What is it you think you did?" Pagara's voice was soft and soothing.

"I stole Kyana's offling. Oh, by the Great Mother, how could I have done something so terrible? Please tell me she is alright. That they both are." Lavke's eyes were filled with genuine panic.

"They are both fine."

"And Ungut. Where is he? Will he ever forgive me? And Joquel?" Lavke started to cry.

"Do not trouble yourself with that right now. Just rest. Whatever happened to you, it has passed."

"How can you be sure? How can I ever be trusted again around any of them?"

"Shhhhh. Please put this out of your mind. Whatever was wrong with you will not return. I believe this nightmare is over. For all of you."

Lavke finished the rest of the water and lay back down.

CHAPTER 8

With research on the bloodlines completed as thoroughly as could be, Kaisak decided it was time to let some of the males pair. He had thought long and hard on this. It was not in their best interests for the males to mate indiscriminately, so he let Jamor and Lahru help him make the best matches among the unattached males and females.

Having selected the candidates, Kaisak called an assembly and asked Okrek, Drub, and Cerus to come to the front. Then Kaisak called out the names of six females and ordered them to the front too.

"Because of the work Lahru and Jamor have been doing, I am allowing some mating to commence. Each of you males and each of you females presents acceptable breeding combinations. There are more females than males, so the males have a choice. I will let Okrek start. Choose your female."

The females looked at each other, then at the rest of the crowd. Some of them reached out for their mothers to come forward to stand with them.

Okrek was confused but was not going to miss his chance to pick first. He knew all the females well, so he walked over and stood in front of the smallest in the group. "I choose Zelose."

Zelose was relieved. She knew Okrek and liked him; he was easygoing and seemed kind-hearted. But she did not understand what it meant.

"Adik'Tar, may I ask a question? Are we to be paired? Is this a permanent match?"

"Yes. Dak'Tor and Iria were paired, as were Dazal and Vaha. It is the best arrangement for our future."

Hearing that, Okrek was relieved he had gotten to choose first. He looked at Zelose and smiled.

She smiled back.

Not one for rituals, Kaisak waved the couple off, indicating that was it.

Okrek took Zelose by the hand and walked to the back of the crowd where her parents were anxiously standing.

Kaisak called on Drub next. He walked over to the five remaining females and looked them over as if inspecting them. Drub was a bit of an attention-getter, and he was never openly mean or cruel, but he was enjoying the limelight, oblivious to what it might be like for the females.

Suddenly, his mother stepped out of the crowd and scuffed him on the back of the head. "Stop it.

You are lucky to be given this honor. Now act respectfully."

The crowd chuckled. Drub's mother was not one to be toyed with, and they respected her for it. It was not that Drub was a bad son, only that he was letting his ego get the better of him.

Drub looked at the females and said, "I am sorry. I would be honored to be with any of you. Would any one of you choose me?"

Unimpressed, Kaisak straightened up and started to step forward. A strong claw-like grasp drew his attention, and he whipped his head around to see Useaves standing behind him.

She frowned and raised a crooked finger. "Stop," she hissed. "You are winning here; learn when to bend."

Kaisak shook her grasp off and pulled himself together.

From the group of females, Midil stepped forward. She had long had a crush on Drub despite his sometimes arrogant ways. Drub took her hand and thanked her, and in turn, led her away.

Last to pick was Cerus, a tall, fine-looking fellow. He was relieved that Utite was still among the four who remained. He had been holding his breath, afraid that one of the others would pick her. He extended his hand, and she readily took it.

Not knowing what would happen next, the other females looked at Kaisak.

"You are free to go back home to your families.

You will be chosen again when you next fall into the pool of acceptable matches. I cannot tell you that the number of females to males will always provide this wide a selection for the males, but we will see."

When the crowd had dispersed, Kaisak turned on Useaves. "Why did you stop me? That was not what I wanted. It was for the males to choose. We will not return to the corrupt ways of the females choosing."

"I could have told you exactly which male and female would have ended up together if you had asked me," Useaves scolded him. "And if you had, you could have been the greatest Leader ever in their eyes for being so wise and thoughtful. Instead, you took a terrible risk of one of the males picking a female of another male's preference and causing division. You were lucky this time. You will not be so lucky the next time."

"What makes you such an expert about this?"

"I know the community. I know each member. I know who likes who and who does not like who. Just as I knew that Visha and Iria did not get along."

"I listened to you on that one, and it was a mistake. It is not good to have irritation in the community. That much I have learned," he snarled.

"I chose Visha for several reasons. That she is Krac's daughter and that it would elevate her status, thus increasing Krac's loyalty to you. The fact that it would cause issues among the younger generation was only one reason."

"Well, you are wrong about Dak'Tor; he is not a threat to me. He agrees that the Akassa and Sassen should be destroyed. For all your *knowing*, you did not take time to find that out. His value is not just as a stronghold over the Guardian should she come to cause trouble or in his role of seeding new offling, but that he is also the key to keeping the entire community united and focused on our true mission."

Useaves could see that arguing with Kaisak was getting her nowhere. She was not sure where her master plan was now. Gard had grown cold and was now one of Kaisak's advisors. Kaisak was smart, and it was much harder to manipulate him than Gard or, previously, Laborn. She needed to re-think her own goals. She could not try to keep Dak'Tor and Kaisak at odds if it would create enmity between her and the current Leader.

"Visha's offling is a male. And he is also Dak'Tor's."

"So?" Kaisak said impatiently. It was only his fear of Useaves that kept him there. He understood now why Laborn had kept her close.

"He could be of great use to you when he is older."

He waited for Useaves to continue.

"Visha will come to resent Dak'Tor now that she has produced the offling and realizes she has no leverage to force him to spend time with her. So Iria will rise above her again since she alone is Dak'Tor's mate. Visha is the only one you can win to your side, as in the end, she will have no loyalty to Dak'Tor."

"Go on." Kaisak was finally admitting his interest in her viewpoint.

"What if, when he is older, you send their son, Moart'Tor, to Kthama. Perhaps in the guise of opening a dialogue between the Guardian and us. It would be obvious to the Guardian that he is Dak'-Tor's son. Of course, Moart'Tor must be raised to know that it was Dak'Tor who seeded his mother. You and Dak'Tor will need to be on good terms with each other, and Dak'Tor and Moart'Tor will have to have a good relationship in order to win over the Guardian. It would be a way for you to find out what is going on there. She must be anxious to hear about her brother and what happened to him and would welcome Moart'Tor as a member of her family. Of course, after he learns what you need to know, he will make an excuse and come back. In return, you will learn the state of their overall community and how large their numbers are compared to the Akassa. Yes?"

Kaisak steepled his fingers together and pressed them against his lips. "And what of the Sassen?"

"We will get them in time. Mothoc will not rise against Mothoc; our blood is too precious to spill. They will have no choice but to let us slaughter the Akassa. Once we have annihilated the Akassa, then we can worry about the Sassen."

"And what of this Promised One?"

"Moart'Tor will also find out about him. What-ever he learns and brings back will be more than we know now."

"So, how do I win over Visha and her son?"

Useaves tried to keep from smiling. "You are not paired, are you? It seems Visha needs a mate and a strong male to help her raise her offling."

Kaisak actually laughed. "And how do I do this without alienating Dak'Tor?"

"Dak'Tor has no interest in Visha. No doubt he is pleased that Dazal and Vaha fell in love. He will gladly step aside and let his friend Dazal raise his son in his stead. I am sure he feels the same about Visha. That way, he can concentrate on his precious Iria. But, as I said, it would behoove you to include him in Moart'Tor's life to ensure an identity as part of the Guardian's family. But a warning; you must make Visha happy. If you do not, you will have a shrew on your hands. I can promise you that."

"Well, since you have all the answers tonight, how do I make Visha happy?"

"Status is the way to win Visha. She will be the mate of the Adik'Tar; that is a good start. Other than that, give her whatever she asks. And be kind to her son. You must commit to raising him, Kaisak. She will see through you if you do not genuinely do right by her son and by her."

He thought of his own father, who abandoned

him and his mother. Kaisak had been a young offling and had vowed that if he were ever a father, he would do better than was done by him.

"I would be using Moart'Tor. Lying to him, sending him to Kthama on a ruse. It would destroy the trust between us. Otherwise, I must ask him outright to lie for us, learn what he can, and return. Our cause is just, but asking him to participate in such deceit could turn him against me."

"You will raise him to understand that our cause *is* just. And that by going to Kthama and returning with crucial information about what is going on there will be his part in helping us succeed. We are trying to save all of Etera and win back the blessing of the Great Spirit. You have time to make him understand that and the importance of his role in it."

"I can do that," Kaisak said, as much to himself as to Useaves. "Tell me, though, while we are talking, how has the training with Iria gone?"

"I am close to having taught her what I know. Then I must test how much she has absorbed and will remember."

"Everything? In so short a time?"

"The basics. The most important treatments for infection, fever, not being able to fall asleep, stomach pain, how to mend cuts, how to poison people."

Kaisak watched the wry smile come over Useaves. He wondered if she knew he had been trying to find that out. "How to poison people? What have you not taught her?"

"Treatments for some of the more infrequent and incidental occasions. For example, the antidote to poisoning someone."

Useaves' grin told Kaisak that she knew what he was getting at.

"After all this time, you still think you can outsmart me," she said. "Do you not think that in the past Laborn asked me to do the same? Select someone and train them? I only agreed to do so now because, in time, I may fall ill and need help. But do not think for a moment that I did not realize your real intent in creating a replacement for me. I have no intention of poisoning you, Kaisak. We need your strength. But you had better stop worrying about me and start thinking about what you will do when the Guardian returns."

"I have already thought about that. I am not foolish enough to believe the Guardian will be less passionate about unifying the Mothoc than I am about destroying the abominations her father created. And you have given me the way to learn what is going on at Kayerm, through Visha and her son Moart'Tor."

Kaisak hated to admit that Useaves was turning out to be a valuable resource after all.

Useaves, of course, had lied about the antidote. If there were antidotes to the poisons she knew of, they were unknown to her. But Kaisak didn't need to know that.

The next few days were filled with joy and celebration. That Kaisak had let some of the community pair put everyone in high spirits.

Kaisak considered everything Useaves had said. He started watching Visha, learning as much as he could about her personality. She did have an edge to her, but that would simply be a challenge and pleasurable in its own way. In the end, he decided he was strong enough to handle her and ultimately tame her.

The Leader was fairly confident that Krac would not object to his daughter being chosen but wanted to be sure.

He decided to take Krac on a hunting trip so he could talk to him away from listening ears.

After a successful day, they lay stretched out on the ground, the last of its summer heat warming their backs as they gazed up at the sprinkling of stars stretched across the dark night sky.

"How is Visha adjusting to motherhood?" Kaisak asked.

"She seems to be happy. Having an offling has softened her some. I do not know how long it will last, though." Krac chuckled. "She has always been a handful. Like her mother."

"What has it been like, being paired to Kerga?"

"There were days I would have liked to wring her neck, and other days I would take a spear to defend her. Usually the former, though. He laughed again. "In all seriousness, I love the fire in her; the fire that burns can also warm. It is a question of handling her passion, for that is what it is. Visha has the same fire."

"That sounds interesting," Kaisak said, still staring at the night sky.

"What?" Krac came up on one elbow, facing Kaisak. "What are you thinking?"

"I am thinking it is time I took a mate."

"And you are considering Visha? She is beautiful, to be sure, and she would eat up being the mate of the Adik'Tar; you can count on that." Krac lay back down.

"What would Kerga think?"

"My mate has the same love of status. She was thrilled when you selected Visha for Dak'Tor to seed. But what of Moart'Tor?"

"I would raise Visha's son as my own. It matters not who seeded him. I would do right by him, I promise you that. And by her."

For the first time, Krac actually saw some humanity in Kaisak. Some vulnerability. He pictured Kaisak and Visha together and chuckled.

"Your life will never be boring; I can promise you that."

Krac tried to stop thinking about the sparks that would no doubt fly between his daughter and Kaisak.

Visha was resentful that the recent pairings had taken the attention away from her and her son. She tried to compensate by parading him through the community. It worked, as the other females were fascinated with his coloring.

Iria was glad of this. As long as Visha was happy, she was not causing trouble for her or Dak'Tor. Iria did worry about how Dak'Tor was going to be a father to so many offling, especially since her mate had told her about Kaisak's plan that he would continue seeding females.

Dazal had joined in the raising of Altka, and the community seemed to accept this arrangement entirely. He was often seen carting Altka around, taking her to visit the beautiful summer blossoms, and now that the leaves were turning again, pointing out each bright new color. She was too young to understand, but she seemed to enjoy Dazal's attentions.

Iria wanted to talk to Vaha to see if her resentment was lessening but couldn't bring herself to do so. She had hoped that time would heal the betrayal that Vaha felt and also hoped that by not bringing it up, the wound might heal. When the group spent time together, Vaha still sat far away from Dazal, even when he was the one holding Altka. Iria was surprised that no one in the community had noticed the estrangement between the two. To her, it was obvious, but perhaps because they both meant so much to her.

One day, however, Dazal's sister Dara brought up the subject. "She seemed happy when he first asked to pair with her, but now she seems like a different person. Distant. As if something heavy is on her mind all the time."

"We must be patient with her," said Iria. "Sometimes we go through these changes after giving birth."

"But Altka is not a newborn. Vaha should be long past that phase by now, should she not?"

"All we can do is continue to include them and hope that if there is something wrong between them, it will work itself out."

"I was talking about Vaha, and now you are talking about her relationship with my brother," Dara said. "Is there something I do not know about?"

Iria had tripped herself up. Secrets were always so very hard to keep without slipping up. She hated deceit and hated to be a part of it, but she would not betray Dak'Tor and Dazal by revealing what had been done.

"Please tell me," Dara pleaded. "I love my brother, and if he is unhappy, I want to know about it,"

"There is nothing that I can tell you," Iria said truthfully. "But he does love Vaha's offling, does he not?"

That brought a smile to Dara's face. "He spends

more time with her than Dak'Tor does, and I do not mean any offense by that."

"I understand. Dak'Tor does not mean to shirk any responsibility, but it is wonderful how it has worked out. Altka has a full-time father, and Vaha has a full-time mate. Dak'Tor would never interfere with that."

"I just wish Vaha felt that way. I am not sure she appreciates what she has," Dara said despondently.

Dara was concerned by Iria's words, and after observing Dazal and Vaha together, decided to get to the bottom of it. She found her brother by following the giggles. He was down by the shallows, dipping Altka's toes in the cool water, which seemed to delight her.

"You were not hard to find," Dara said as she approached. Her brother looked up at her with a big smile on his face.

"We are just having some fun."

"I can see that. You love her so much."

He grimaced at the offling, making her laugh all over again. "Do you want to hold her?" he asked.

"Any chance I can!" Dara answered and leaned over to take Altka.

"You were looking for me; what is it about?" he asked, standing up.

"I have not talked to you privately for a while. I wanted to ask how everything is between you and Vaha. You two do not seem as close as you did before you were paired. Is something wrong? There must be," Dara said.

"Sometimes, it just takes a while to get used to living with another person."

Dara looked at him disbelievingly. "It is more than that. It has to be. Please tell me what is going on. Maybe I can help?"

Altka entertained herself by tugging on Dara's hair.

"No, that is not something to eat," Dara explained as she gently pulled it away from Altka's little hands just as the offling was about to chew on it.

"Thank you for your concern, but it just has to work its way out. Are our parents asking about it?"

"No. All they see is how much Altka loves you. They accept her as if she were yours."

"She is mine," Dazal said.

"I know." Dara smiled. "It does not matter who seeded her. You are her father; that is obvious to everyone."

"Just be patient. Be kind to Vaha."

"Please tell me what is wrong. I can see the distance between you when we are all together."

Dazal looked away. "I made a terrible mistake, and it hurt her very badly. She needs time to forgive me. She is doing the best she can. We both are."

Dara realized that was as much as her brother was going to tell her, but at least she knew it was not her imagination. She kissed Altka on the forehead and handed her back to Dazal. "See you at evening meal, I hope."

Dara had not meant to seek her out but ran into Vaha on the way back. "Dak'Tor is down at the shallows with your daughter," Dara said, pointing back the way she had just come.

"Thank you; I know. I can hear Altka laughing."

"He truly loves her. And he loves you too," Dara said.

"I do know that."

"In one way, it is none of my business, but in another way, it is. He is my brother, and I love him dearly, and though he won't say what it is, he knows he made some dreadful mistake and hurt you badly."

"It is complicated."

"Is it? What I see is a male who loves his mate and has apologized and is treating her with respect, kindness, and devotion. A male who has accepted her offling as if she were his own. I do not know a female here who would not fall on her knees with gratitude for such love."

"Things happened. Things that you do not know about."

"Well, my question to you is this; at what point

are you going to forgive him for whatever you are punishing him for? Are you going to make him pay his whole life? And what of your daughter? He clearly loves her, and she loves him. What happens when she grows up and sees the distance between you? She has a chance to have a father who is committed to her and wants to spend time with her. Are you also going to make her pay for his crime, whatever that was, with her happiness?"

Vaha stood with her mouth open, probably at being spoken to so frankly.

"You can be mad at me for talking to you like this, but someone has to. You are throwing away my brother's happiness and your own. As well as your daughter's. If you truly hate him so much, then you should release him and let him find someone else. Though I do not know what that would do to your daughter. But I guess that is not your problem."

Dara waited for her to say something, but Vaha just turned her back. Dara threw her arms up in the air and walked off.

Huge tears streamed down Vaha's face. Everything Dara had just said hit her hard because it was all true. She was punishing Dazal. She was punishing them all, Dazal, Dak'Tor, Iria. But she had not thought of what it could be doing to Altka. Or would do, in time.

Her bitterness was hurting everyone, including herself.

Vaha had intended to retrieve Altka from Dazal, but instead, she turned down a different path and went off by herself.

CHAPTER 9

It was almost time for the pairing ceremony. Kant had helped Wry'Wry pack up the tools she was bringing to trade. Not sure what she would be able to trade them for, and because it was an experiment, she only took a few. She was looking forward to seeing her parents and Tensil. She wondered if anything more had come of Tensil's contact with the Brothers' Healer. She was looking forward to every part of the visit—except seeing Takthan'Tor.

Many of the people from the little community were going. Not only did they have more females who had asked to be paired, but it was a time for everyone to socialize. All knew that their Adik'Tar, Tar'Kahn, had joined with Gontis'Rar, Leader of the Little River, and sent out searchers to see if they could find the Protectors. They were hoping to learn if that party had returned with any good news. It was one of the few topics that brightened their spirits.

"Are you ready to go?" Kant asked.

Wry'Wry nodded. Their relationship was still estranged.

"I need to speak with you before we leave."

Her heart sank. *Now what?* But she knew. It was just that talking about it did not seem to help anything.

"You are not happy here. Everyone sees it. Whatever the reason, I do not think it is going to get any better for you. For us. I need to let you know that I am going to ask the High Council for Bak'tah-Awhidi."

Wry'Wry's mouth fell open. "You want our pairing set aside?"

"Yes. I am not going to blame you. If they need verification, Tar'Kahn will speak for us. You look shocked," he added.

"I suppose I am. I know neither of us is happy; I just did not think it would come to this."

"You are young and beautiful. And not seeded. You and I both have a chance at finding someone who will love us as it should be."

"You have been nothing but kind to me, Kant, and patient. The fault is not yours."

"It was just not a good match, no one's fault, and I wish you only the best. So if you want to pack your personal belongings and return to live at the High Rocks, we still have time."

Oh no, Wry'Wry thought. But there was no place else for her to go. "Yes. Thank you. It was kind of you to let me know ahead of time. As far as the rest of my tools go—"

"I can have them brought along."

"Thank you. I know you do not need them here, or I would just leave them."

That afternoon, Kant and Wry'Wry set out with all those from their community who were traveling to the High Rocks. And while Wry'Wry had been looking forward to this visit, now it was no longer a visit. It was a return home.

Wry'Wry's parents were thrilled to hear that she was coming to Kthama. Vor'Ran had prepared rooms nearby for all of them—for her and Kant, as well as Kant's parents. Though it had not been that long since her visit with her daughter, Tlanik was hoping to see that Wry'Wry was happier.

Persica had been excited to see Wry'Wry again, but now she had figured out that Wry'Wry was in love with Takthan'Tor, and she was not sure how her friend would take the news that they were to be paired. She knew it was customary that no one should know the Leader's choice of mate before the ceremony, but she did not want Wry'Wry to be blind-sided in public.

Watchers had sent word that the visitors from the

little community would arrive in the early evening. Persica and Wry'Wry's mother were waiting anxiously, and just as they sat down for evening meal, Wry'Wry, Kant, and Kant's parents walked into the Great Chamber. Persica jumped up and moved quickly to her friend, inviting everyone to join their table

"We will come back later and see if you are still here. We just arrived and need to settle in," Wry'Wry explained.

"Of course. Since you did not have anything with you, I thought you had perhaps been here a while," Persica said.

"No, my father met us and arranged help with taking our things to our quarters. I just came in to see if my mother was here. I am glad to see you too, though!" And Wry'Wry embraced first her mother and then Persica.

She turned to leave, but as she did, Persica noticed that she quickly scanned the room. She must be looking for Takthan'Tor.

It was the following morning, and Kthama was bustling with activity. Takthan'Tor was relieved to see how many had come for the Ashwea Awhidi, not least because a High Council meeting was planned following the pairings.

The time was drawing close, and as they stood

together waiting to greet the next arrivals,
Takthan'Tor decided to tell Vor'Ran that he was
taking a mate. It might be customary that no one
should know, but the Leader's most trusted relationship was with Vor'Ran, who had been encouraging
him to be paired, and Takthan'Tor felt he should tell
him upfront.

"I am to be paired tomorrow with Persica from
the Far High Hills."

Instead of the reaction Takthan'Tor had
expected, Vor'Ran just stared at him blankly. He
eventually said, "She will make a fine mate. She is
smart, and she will be a good helper to you and
provide wise counsel."

"I expected a more hearty reaction," Takthan'Tor
said. "It is you and Tensil who have been the loudest
proponents of my being paired."

"It is the right thing to do; I am just not sure she
is the one for you."

Takthan'Tor frowned. "In what way? You just said
she is smart and will be a great help to me. What
more is there?"

"You know the answer to that. You yourself have
often spoken of the legendary love between Moc'Tor
and E'ranale. Between Straf'Tor and Ushca. It seems
you are settling."

Takthan'Tor slammed his fist down on a nearby
table. "By the Great Spirit! What do you want from
me? First, you push me to be paired, and then you
find fault with my choice."

It was uncharacteristic of Takthan'Tor to lose his temper.

"What I want is to see you light up when you speak of her. That you search the room for her face when you enter. That the mate you choose is not just chosen by your reason, because it is a wise choice, but because she makes your heart sing when you hear her name and pound wildly when you take her in your arms. I see nothing of that spark between you and Persica."

"Do you have another idea?" Takthan'Tor replied.

"I did. At one time. But it does not matter now."

Takthan'Tor brusquely walked off and then turned back just as abruptly. "No. You brought this up. So speak your mind!"

"All right. There was a time when I was sure that you and my daughter would end up paired. And then it all changed. You cooled toward her. She noticed it. I noticed it. We all did. And neither Tlanik nor I know why."

Takthan'Tor ran his hand through the thick silver crown of his hair and down the back of his head. "This is a nightmare."

"Is it? If you say that, then you must still have feelings for Wry'Wry."

"Of course I still have feelings for Wry'Wry. She was the one who touched my heart at a level I never thought possible. Who offered the once-in-a-lifetime romance I had longed for all my growing years. I wanted to pair with her, but I did not because of my responsibilities as Leader of the High Rocks."

"What responsibilities are you talking about?"

"To be fair and just. To do the best by our people that I can. And that includes choosing a mate who will provide balance to the circle of leadership. How could I have made Wry'Wry Third Rank when she is your daughter, and you are my High Protector?"

"That is the most un-wise thing I have ever heard you say. But then that is how females can affect us, I guess?"

Takthan'Tor stared at him.

"A Leader has to be all those things, yes," Vor'Ran continued. "Fair. Balanced. Unbiased. But he also has to be happy. The correct pairing is the greatest blessing. It is the foundation that affects us each in the deepest way. Love is the essence of each of us, even though we may not always act like it. We are created from the love of the Great Spirit, and it is love which brings us home to our best and truest nature."

"I do love Persica."

"I am sure you do. But not like you loved Wry'Wry."

"I will never feel about another female the way I did about Wry'Wry. This is the best choice for me."

"And what about Persica?"

"She understands. She knows about my feelings for Wry'Wry."

"She deserves better than that, Takthan'Tor. I speak to you not only as your High Protector but as a father and your friend. I urge you to wait until you feel for another as you felt for my daughter."

"It will never happen, Vor'Ran. Never. I thank you for your counsel, but it is too late. Wry'Wry is paired to Kant, and after tonight, Persica will be my mate and serve at my side as High Rock's Third Rank."

Vor'Ran sighed heavily. "You are my Adik'Tar. It is my duty to tell you when I think you are making a mistake. I will stand by you, no matter what, but I fear you will live to regret this."

Vor'Ran watched Takthan'Tor leave. He was torn. Did he tell Tlanik of this? Despite Takthan'Tor's words, Vor'Ran knew that the Leader was still in love with Wry'Wry. How sadly this had all turned out. Perhaps if he and Tlanik had not pushed Wry'Wry so, it would have come to light, and he and Takthan'Tor could have had this conversation earlier.

Vor'Ran did not know that the Leader was at all likely to hold out until he found another who moved him as deeply as Wry'Wry had. In fact, despite their conversation, he had to assume not since the Leader had said his pairing was still going to take place.

While waiting for the afternoon to pass, Takthan'Tor came across Tar'Kahn and Gontis'Rar speaking together. "May I join you? I am wondering if your sentries have returned with any news of the Protectors?"

Gontis'Rar answered, "No. Mine have not. They followed the magnetic lines in several directions but with no luck. It only makes sense that wherever the Protectors went, they would be looking for a strong vortex."

"That does make sense. And you?" Takthan'Tor asked, turning to Tar'Kahn.

"No success, either. But we are not giving up. I will send others out eventually. It is the only way to turn this around."

"Turn what around?" Takthan'Tor asked.

"This decline we are in. I know you see it; you have mentioned it. Our people are deteriorating. Yes, there is laughter and happiness here, but that is because of the joy of this one event. Once it is over, they will return to their lives of discontent. It is no use; we cannot overcome it. How can we, when we, their Leaders suffer from it ourselves."

Takthan'Tor was tired of fighting them. His only help lay with the Great Spirit. Surely there was a plan that had taken this into consideration. In his heart, he prayed again for help, for anything to save his people from the downward spiral they were in. Without an intervention, the future of their making looked destined to be bleak.

Persica had finally found time to talk to Wry'Wry. She wanted to explain that she and Takthan'Tor were to be paired.

"I am so glad you are here. Did you bring your tools?"

"Yes. And more."

"And more?" Persica chuckled. Then she looked serious. "Are things any better with Kant?" She wanted to be polite and ask her friend about herself first.

"No. They are not. In fact, there is another reason why we are here besides my wanting to trade my cutting tools. Kant is going to ask the High Council for Bak'tah-Awhidi."

Persica froze. "He is going to set aside your pairing?"

"It is mutual. I cannot adjust to life there, and I miss home terribly, but the fault is not his. I hope he finds someone else, someone who will love him as he deserves to be loved. As Moc'Tor loved E'ranale. As I loved—"

"Oh no," Persica said. "Oh, Wry'Wry. I wanted to talk to you because you are my friend, but I also wanted to tell you that Takthan'Tor and I are to be paired tonight."

Wry'Wry looked away. Suddenly she had to squeeze her eyes to stop the tears. "I am happy for you; you are a good choice for him. I pray you will both have the love you deserve."

"Thank you. But what horrible timing," Persica said.

"Why do you say that? Our request for Bak'tah-Awhidi will happen after the Ashwea Awhidi; it will not affect the ceremony tonight."

"Wry'Wry, I know it is Takthan'Tor you are in love with. If you wish, I will go to him and stop our pairing."

Wry'Wry turned to look at Persica. "Oh no! Do not do such a thing. You will be great together. You are both wise and understanding, and you will help him lead the High Rocks better than anyone. Whatever was once between Takthan'Tor and me, its chance has passed. It is over. Go and start your life with him. Be happy. Have lots of little Takthan'Tors," and the smallest of smiles crossed her lips.

Persica leaned over and hugged her friend tight. "If you change your mind, let me know. There is still time."

"I will not. If it was what the Great Spirit wanted, we would not be in this situation. Look at the timing; you and Takthan'Tor are to be paired the night before my pairing with Kant is dissolved. It is obvious it just was not meant to be."

Persica sat quietly with Wry'Wry for some time before leaving. She knew they all deserved to be happy, and she and Takthan'Tor no less than anyone else. Wry'Wry was right. Look how it had all turned out. Surely if it was meant to be, it would have fallen into place for them.

It was time. Takthan'Tor took his place at the front of the room, standing on the speaking platform. He looked out over the crowd. So many familiar faces. At the very back sat Vor'Ran and Tlanik with Tar'Kahn next to them. Just then, Persica and Culrat'Sar entered, and Takthan'Tor turned his attention to them. They walked to the front and took a seat where he had asked them to.

Takthan'Tor raised his hand to speak. He made a striking figure with his muscular build, strong features, and the wide swath of silver hair adorning his crown. "Welcome, everyone, to our second Ashwea Awhidi. We have quite a few pairings to conduct, so I will call those selected to the front.

He called up each couple individually. They came forward, and one by one, Takthan'Tor pronounced Ashwea Awhidi over them. In between, there was chatter and smiling at the joyful event until, finally, it was the end.

It was time for Takthan'Tor to announce his pairing. He looked down at the front row and smiled at Persica. She smiled back, waiting for his signal to come forward. When he motioned for her, she rose and walked to the front to take her place at his side.

Just as she turned to face the crowd, Persica noticed Takthan'Tor's head turn. At the very back, Wry'Wry and Kant had entered and were taking a seat next to his parents and their Leader, Tar'Kahn.

Takthan'Tor froze.

Persica turned to look at him.

He shook his head and looked down at her. "I am sorry, I was distracted. He turned back to the crowd, "People of the High Rocks, the Far High Hills, the Little River, the Deep Valley, Tar'Kahn's community, as Leader of Kthama, I am given the right to choose my own mate. It is my honor to announce—"

"Wait," said Persica.

Takthan'Tor looked at her.

"Wait. Please, stop."

Time itself seemed to stop, as if even the birds of the air were frozen in mid-flight.

Persica looked up at Takthan'Tor with tears in her eyes. "I am sorry. I am sorry, but I cannot let you do this. In many ways, we are a great match. But it is not my face you search the crowd for. And it is not my heart that starts yours pounding when I walk in. It is Wry'Wry you love. I know it, and you know it. It is time you tell her, Takthan'Tor. It is time you be honest about how you feel about her."

"What are you doing?" Takthan'Tor bent down and whispered. "Whatever I felt or feel for Wry'Wry has no bearing on you and me."

"Oh, but it does, and it always will," she whispered back. "You deserve better. And so do I. I would never be your First Choice. I thought I could live with it, but I cannot. Go to her, tell her how you really feel; she deserves to know the truth."

"Please, can we not do this in front of everyone?"

His voice unwittingly rose. "She is paired to Kant, and I love you, Persica."

"I know, but not as you love her. She came here to trade her tools, but there is another reason they are here. They are approaching the High Council tomorrow to ask for Bak'tah-Awhidi. From you, as Overseer. I thought you should know."

Takthan'Tor's mind was reeling. Wry'Wry would be free. They could still be paired. But why now? Why did all of this have to come out now?

"It is not meant to be. The Order of Functions brought us here, you and me," Takthan'Tor said.

"What has brought us to this moment is your stubbornness. If you had told Wry'Wry of your feelings, I would not be standing here now; she would."

The crowd was drowning in questions, but no one dared speak. What was unfolding before them was mesmerizing, if not heartbreaking.

Vor'Ran's words came back to Takthan'Tor.

"What I want is to see you light up when you speak of her. That you search the room for her face when you enter. That the mate you choose is not just chosen by your reason because it is a wise choice, but because she makes your heart sing when you hear her name and pound wildly when you take her in your arms. I see nothing of that spark between you and Persica."

Vor'Ran was right. Persica was a great choice. But she would be his First Choice in title only.

Takthan'Tor turned his attention back to her.

"Go," she said. "I will be fine. Stand in truth

about your feelings for her. Stand in the presence of the Great Spirit and let happen whatever is meant to be. Now, in front of everyone, you must risk setting this right."

He leaned over and kissed her on the forehead, and briefly caressed her face. Then he stepped down off the platform and headed to the back of the room.

Wry'Wry had stalled until the last moment before entering the Ashwea Awhidi. She knew that Takthan'Tor and Persica would be paired as the last event. Part of her wanted to skip it, but a stronger part believed it was what she needed to finally get Takthan'Tor out of her heart. She needed to be there.

When Wry'Wry came in with Kant, and she saw Persica standing next to Takthan'Tor, it was all she could do not to sob out loud. And then, suddenly, it all stopped. Takthan'Tor left the platform and started heading toward the back of the room; for some reason, he must be leaving.

And then she realized he was heading straight for her.

Every head turned to follow the Leader to where he stopped in the aisle in front of Wry'Wry.

Takthan'Tor turned to look at Kant, unsure of what to say.

After meeting Takthan'Tor's eyes, Kant glanced across at Wry'Wry. Then he stood up and announced, "What Persica said is true. Wry'Wry and I came here to ask the High Council for Bak'tah-Awhidi tomorrow. Our pairing was a mistake. It is no one's fault. There is no one to blame. And there is no shame in acknowledging what we both know in our hearts and souls to be true."

Kant turned to Wry'Wry and offered her his hand to help her to her feet. "Now I understand. I am sorry for what you have gone through, but I am relieved to know the truth. There is no way you could have loved me with someone else in your heart."

"I am sorry. I am sorry I have hurt you," Wry'Wry said.

Kant wiped the tears from her cheeks. "You have not hurt me. It is as Persica said; you deserve better, and so do I. And as of tomorrow, we will be free to find out what paths will bring us to that."

He looked at Takthan'Tor. "But I think yours is pretty obvious at this point," and he smiled, which freed Wry'Wry's heart from the anguish it was in.

Then Kant stepped out of her way, "Go to him, Wry'Wry. Go to your true love. May we all be so blessed to find what you two have together."

Wry'Wry gave Kant a nod and stepped out into the aisle to stand in front of Takthan'Tor. He said her name, and she felt faint.

"Wry'Wry, I have been a fool. In trying to be the best Leader I could be, I almost made the biggest mistake of my life. I have loved you for some time. When you paired with Kant, I thought that was the end of it; you were lost to me forever, and I only wanted for you to be happy, to find the love you deserve. I tried to make peace with it; I tried to move on, and that is when Persica and I decided to be paired." Takthan'Tor turned back to look at Persica, still standing at the front but now joined by her father, Culrat'Sar.

"Persica is a wonderful soul. She is wise and kind, and she will make the perfect mate for someone. But in her wisdom, she realizes it is not me. I love you, Wry'Wry. I ask you to be my First Choice."

Wry'Wry's hand flew to her mouth as the entire assembly broke out in commotion.

Culrat'Sar, who had been standing with his arm around his daughter, stepped forward. "What is the meaning of this. What are you talking about? You and my daughter are to be paired, and Wry'Wry is already paired to Kant. You pronounced them paired yourself. Have you lost your senses?"

"Father, no," Persica said. "He has not lost his senses; he has come to them. It will be alright, I promise."

Wry'Wry smiled at Takthan'Tor. "I love you," she said, "and I always will. Ask me again tomorrow."

Takthan'Tor laughed, and then it seemed that all the members of the High Rocks community broke out cheering. He looked around, surprised.

"You thought none of us knew what was going on all this time?" someone shouted.

"Yes! Thank the Great Spirit that you two finally figured it out!" another voice called out.

Takthan'Tor and Wry'Wry just looked at each other and laughed.

"Well, I guess we do not have to worry what the others will think of our pairing," she said.

The Leader leaned over and placed a kiss on her cheek. "Till tomorrow, then."

Persica raised her hands in the air and shouted, "What are we doing all standing around? This is a celebration, so let us celebrate!"

The room came alive with movement as everyone seemed to leave their places at once. There was a flurry of congratulations and more laughter, and quite a few people drying their eyes.

Culrat'Sar made his way to Takthan'Tor and Wry'Wry, who were still standing together.

"I asked you once not to hurt my daughter," he said.

Takthan'Tor waited.

"And she tells me you have not. My daughter is a remarkable female. She has more faith in the Order of Functions than most of us.

"We owe her more than we can ever repay her," Wry'Wry said.

"You do not have to worry about that. The Great Spirit has a way of making these things work out." And Culrat'Sar left to be with his daughter, who already had a crowd encircling her.

The gathering went on into the night, and

Takthan'Tor and Wry'Wry walked around among the crowd, not in any hurry to retire, knowing that neither would sleep much tonight.

Tlanik and Vor'Ran waited until most of the crowd had cleared before going to their daughter. Tlanik held Wry'Wry close and whispered in her ear, "I am so happy for you both. Kant seems to be taking it well, as does Persica."

"They are both wonderful souls. I hope they find the true love they both deserve," said Wry'Wry.

"Since you no doubt do not want to spend the night with Kant, would you like to stay with us?" her mother asked. "It will be like old times."

"Yes, that would be perfect, but let me check with Kant. I do not want to leave him alone on our last night together if it will hurt him."

Kant did not mind. "Go and be with your family. Our life together is ending, but that just means the future is open to whatever is meant to be instead. I wish you only the best."

So Wry'Wry spent the night with her parents; the last night before starting her life paired to the male she had thought lost to her forever.

CHAPTER 10

Visha knew something was up, but she could not put her finger on it. She knew Kaisak was watching her but had no idea why. Finally, she confronted him.

"Why do you keep watching me? I can think of nothing I have done wrong."

"You have done nothing wrong. I simply find you —interesting."

"You have known me all my life. Why am I now suddenly interesting?"

"I imagine it is because you are no longer an offling," and he looked her up and down.

If Visha could have blushed, she would have; she could feel her face burning. It was not like it for a male to unnerve her.

"Come and sit with me at the fire tonight," he said.

Visha was not sure if it was an order; it almost

sounded like a request, and she thought for a moment. "I will be there. What of my son, Moart'Tor?"

"I expect you would bring him unless it is too late for him to be awake. I do not know of these things."

"I will see you later."

Useaves waited until Visha had left and appeared as if from nowhere, startling Kaisak.

"Do not sneak up on me, old female," he admonished her, addressing her as Laborn often had.

"I was not sneaking up on you. If you had not been staring at Visha as she walked away, you would have heard me. So she does interest you."

"She does. For once, you have made a wise suggestion."

Useaves let it go without a retort but gave a little chuckle as she went on her way.

Evening came soon enough. As usual, nearly all the community was gathered. The fire was comforting, creating a cozy dome of light under the dark cover of night. It was early enough that some of the offling were there with their parents.

Sometimes there was a lot of talk, but this night it was quiet. People seemed to be enjoying the cooler temperatures and the promise of the refreshing cold weather of the wintertime to come.

Visha did as Kaisak had asked and sat next to

him. After she was seated, her father, Krac, joined them, sitting on her other side. To anyone watching, other than Useaves, it simply looked like a father and daughter sitting together, and it was customary for Krac to sit near the Adik'Tar, just as it was for Gard.

Krac poked at the fire, making embers flare. The offling laughed and pointed at the fiery display drifting skyward.

Because the community was too large to fit directly around the one firepit, there were rows spread out radiating backward. Though it was mostly quiet, Kaisak made small talk with Visha and Krac.

Dak'Tor and his group had settled in somewhere toward the back, also sitting quietly, each lost in their own thoughts. Dak'Tor looked up as Vaha walked by with Altka.

Unnerved by what Dara had said, Vaha had not waited for Dazal to come with her. Instead, she headed for the front and sat next to her parents. Knowing how much the fire transfixed Altka, they made a space for her.

Altka had started to walk, so they kept a tight grip on the offling. Vaha was happy that the fire delighted her daughter so, but she was eminently aware of the danger it also presented.

Altka waved her chubby hands at the fire as if trying to grab fistfuls of it. Then she was suddenly distracted and started to cry.

"Oh, shhhhh. What is the matter? What is wrong, little one?" Vaha tried to comfort her daughter.

Altka started struggling and twisting her head around. "She is looking for something back there," Vaha's mother said. "What could it be?"

Just then, Altka spotted Dazal. And he spotted her. The moment their eyes met, she spoke her first words, "Papa! Papa!" and reached back toward him, making the same little grabbing motions with her fists as she did when she wanted something.

Vaha's heart melted. Dazal was Altka's father. And she knew it. Not because she knew that he had seeded her mother, but because of how he loved her and cared for her. And in that moment, all Vaha's bitterness melted too, shed and running off like the winter snows.

"Is that who you want?" she asked her daughter. "Papa?" Vaha looked back at Dazal, and then she slowly got up and carried the offling to him.

Dazal stood to take Altka as Vaha handed her over. Altka giggled with joy and grabbed onto his long beard.

"She called me Papa," he said.

"Yes."

Dazal smiled at the sweet offling tugging on his beard.

"Because that is who you are," said Vaha.

Dazal looked up, surprised.

"Oh, Dazal." Vaha dropped to her knees in front of him. "I love you, and I accept your apology. We are a family, and I promise that from now on, it will be different. It will be as it should be between us." She reached out and put her hand on Dazal's arm.

Most of those who overheard them assumed that Dazal and Vaha were making up after one of the usual rough patches relationships went through, but Dak'Tor squeezed Iria's hand, and Dara took Altka from her brother.

Dazal immediately stood up, pulling Vaha into his arms and kissing her. She kissed him back passionately. Then, as Dazal held her tightly in his embrace, Vaha looked over his shoulder and mouthed a thank you to Dara.

Altka reached out her hands toward her parents, her little fingers once again grabbing at the air.

That night, a new life started for Dazal and Vaha.

As the fire was dying down, Kaisak turned to Visha and asked her to stay and talk to him after the others had left.

Once they were alone, he told her, "I would like to spend time with you."

Visha frowned, "Why? Again, I do not understand why I am drawing your attention."

"I will be blunt. I need a mate. And as I said, you interest me."

Visha was not the type to be surprised, but this admission caught her off guard. "You are the Adik'-

Tar. You do not need my permission. You can order me to let you mount me."

"I do not want to order you. I want you to submit to me willingly, as you did to Dak'Tor."

"I did not submit willingly to Dak'Tor," she disagreed.

"And yet you bore his offling."

"I only submitted to his mounting me because my Leader ordered me to," she said.

"You boasted of his mounting you."

"Of course I did. It raised my status. Did you expect I would act otherwise, especially in the face of Dak'Tor's continual insipid fawning over Iria? It is humiliating to be given to a male, any male, only for his pleasure and as a vessel for his seed. But as I said, you ordered me to. "

"I am surprised at your loyalty," Kaisak said.

"People judge me harshly because I do not get along with Iria. But that is between her and me."

"So you want me to bear your offling?" she asked, still trying to understand what was going on.

"I want more than that. I am not ignorant of the pleasures between a male and a female, but I want more than a release and offling. I want a partner. I want a family. I want someone I can talk to, someone to stand by me."

"You have Gard and my father."

"I want someone warm and yielding beside me at night. Someone to talk to in the dark hours. Someone I trust."

"I cannot imagine Laborn ever saying such things," Visha said almost absent-mindedly.

"Laborn loved Shikrin. It destroyed him when she was killed. I believe now that his mind started to decline after that. But I am not Laborn. For a while, I believed, as he did, that dissension was good within the community. That divided people were easier to monitor as infighting kept their attention on each other and not on the Leader. But in order to rule that way, pressure must be continuously applied to maintain the division. I am not sure now. This is why I need someone to help me think through these issues."

"And you think I am that person."

"Tell me, what is the cause of the strain between you and Iria?

Visha did not want to tell Kaisak, but he had been candid and seemingly vulnerable with her, and she felt she had to. "When we were little, Iria was the favorite. The most thoughtful. The most attractive. Everyone wanted to be her friend, play with her. She was always the center of attention. I resented it. I know it sounds immature, but that is how it was."

"As my mate, you would be the center of attention."

Visha looked him up and down. She had to admit he was a comely male, and his status and authority made him all that more attractive to her. However, she was not yet convinced. "We have not talked about my son. What of him?"

"It matters not to me who seeded him. I would care for Moart'Tor and protect him as my own."

Visha wanted to change the subject. "You agree, as Laborn did, that the Akassa and Sassen should be eliminated."

"We lost favor with the Great Spirit. We should have fought Moc'Tor instead of letting ourselves be thrown out, but Norcab was our Leader. He was so strong, and when Moc'Tor killed him, it shook us to the core. Then Moc'Tor banished us from Kthama. We moved to Kayerm, and then Straf'Tor evicted us from there. Then the cave system where Shikrin and others were killed. Now here. We will not find favor with the Great Spirit until we right Moc'Tor's mistakes and return to our rightful home."

"So it is not just about the annihilation of the Akassa and Sassen?"

"No. That is part of it, but once the Akassa are killed, we will retake Kthama. And then the Great Spirit will smile upon us once again."

"So you will be Leader of the High Rocks."

"No."

Visha squinted at him. "Then who?"

"Your son. Only a 'Tor should rule Kthama."

"But what of Dak'Tor. Is he not the rightful 'Tor to sit at the head of the High Rocks?"

"Not as I see it. He can take his inner circle to the smaller cave system at the High Rocks if he wishes. Where the females used to live."

"I am not sure Dak'Tor will agree. Nor will the Guardian."

"That is why I need a mate. I need someone to discuss these issues with. Someone I know who is loyal and will keep it between ourselves. I trust your father, but it is not the same thing."

Visha sighed. "I know. I do understand what you are saying."

"As for the Guardian, her thinking was warped by her father. She is misguided, as most people with a consuming cause can be. She does not understand that by protecting the Akassa and the Sassen, she is perpetuating abominations that should never have been brought into being."

"I am willing to spend time with you. If you are serious about not just ordering me to pair with you, let us first see if we are compatible. Now it is late, and I need to take my son home."

"Of course. Perhaps tomorrow we can take a stroll."

As Dak'Tor lay awake enjoying the soft breathing of his beloved next to him, he thought of his sister's faith in the Order of Functions. He reflected back on all he had been through. The years of rejecting his father's counsel, even the time Moc'Tor wanted to spend with him. All his laziness about learning what every male was expected to learn, how to be a good provider, how to protect his family if need be. How unfair he had been to Ei'Tol, rejecting her when she became pregnant with their daughter, blaming her for asking for Bak'tah-Awhidi when she had every right to. As a mate, he had failed her in every way. And the terrible crime he had committed against his sister, not only in moving the Leader's Staff to her quarters but in stealing the sacred crystal that was stored within it. All his failings; there were so many of them, and yet by some great mercy, he had still found love. He had a family he would kill to protect. He had friends. He had a life that was far more rewarding than any he had imagined for himself at Kthama. Whatever harm had befallen him had been caused by himself and himself alone.

In the dark sanctity of the night, he prayed to the Great Spirit. This time not just for forgiveness, but that he would grow to be worthy of the great blessings that had come his way, blessings he did not deserve but for which he was deeply grateful. And as he had done before, he prayed that someday he would see Pan again and that she would forgive him for everything he had done to her.

CHAPTER 11

Takthan'Tor spent a fitful night. He was overcome with gratitude at how the evening turned out. He and his beloved Wry'Wry were to be paired the next evening after he, as Overseer, had granted Bak'tah-Awhidi to her and Kant. He thought of Persica, who had accepted it all so graciously. He wished only the best for her, and he realized that it was as she had said. Had it not been for his keeping his concerns to himself, everything could have been avoided by talking to Vor'Ran about his daughter, to begin with.

Morning came, and he fought his longing to immediately seek out Wry'Wry. He knew his was the somber duty of declaring Bak'tah-Awhidi and did not want to be irreverent about it. Wry'Wry had not gotten much rest either. She and her parents had stayed up, sharing their excitement about how it had all worked out. They repeatedly lifted praise to the

Great Spirit for the mercy and love they had been shown.

When Takthan'Tor finally walked through the halls of the High Rocks, however, his plans for lying low were immediately forfeited. Everywhere he went, well-wishers came up to him and told him how happy they were for him and Wry'Wry. As many had expressed the night before, some told him how they had watched the blossoming romance between him and Wry'Wry and how sad they were when it seemed to fall apart for no reason they could understand. He was grateful for their outpouring of support.

Despite the amount of activity, the day dragged by until finally, it was time for the High Council meeting. The first order of business was the dissolution of Kant's pairing with Wry'Wry.

Takthan'Tor's heart skipped a beat when he saw his beloved was there, standing in the back next to Kant. "Let us begin the High Council meeting. We will discharge any personal matters so our guests can leave and the official discussions can begin." He looked at Kant and motioned him to come forward.

"You are here to ask for Bak'tah-Awhidi."

"Yes. Both my mate, Wry'Wry, and I wish for our pairing to be set aside." Kant looked back at Wry'Wry, "There are no villains; it was simply not a good match. We part on good terms with no animosity between us."

"Very well. As Overseer of the High Council, I grant you Bak'tah-Awhidi."

"Thank you. And in return, I wish you and Wry'Wry all the best." Kant reached out in a bold move and placed his hand on Takthan'Tor's shoulder.

The Leader smiled at Kant and returned his gesture of brotherhood. "Go in peace," Takthan'Tor said, but could not stop himself from looking back at Wry'Wry.

Kant turned and quietly left. Wry'Wry followed him outside.

"Thank you. Will you be returning home today?" she asked.

"No," Kant said. "My parents and I will wait until after your ceremony. We all support your pairing and feel we need to stay as a show of support and to make sure any rumor of hard feelings is headed off."

It was time for the closing ceremonies. The first order of business was the pairing of Takthan'Tor and Wry'Wry. Because Takthan'Tor was the Overseer, he would have to announce Ashwea Awhidi himself. He called Wry'Wry to the front to stand in front of him. He took both his hands in hers and said, "For a long time, I dreamed of this moment, of you standing in front of me waiting to be paired. And then I let my foolishness push us apart. I did not seek the counsel of others, and we have both paid for that mistake. Forgive me, Saraste'. Forgive me, and let me make it up to you with my devotion for the rest of our lives."

Wry'Wry looked at him and said, "The fault is not yours alone. I should have trusted what I thought was between us. Forgive me as well. And I will show you the same devotion in return, as that is what has always been in my heart."

Takthan'Tor lifted their right hands, still clasped, and announced, "Ashwea Awhidi!"

The entire assembly broke out in laughter and cheers. The paired couple turned to face them, both marveling at the outpouring of love and support.

"As that is the last item to be taken care of, I pronounce this assembly completed," Takthan'Tor announced. "Return to your homes as you will, under the loving care and protection of the Great Spirit."

In the back stood Kant with his parents. Next to them stood Persica with her parents. As everyone started to mingle, Kant turned to Persica.

"May I speak freely?" he asked.

"Of course."

"No one could have handled this situation with as much grace and forgiveness as you did. You are a female among females."

"You have been kind and understanding yourself. It is obvious that you are happy for Takthan'Tor and Wry'Wry, and that speaks highly of you as well."

"Perhaps I could walk you to your quarters?"

"I would enjoy that."

As they walked away, Kant asked her, "How do you feel about small communities?"

Takthan'Tor and Wry'Wry mingled until they felt it was appropriate to leave, and then they walked together toward the Leader's Quarters. From this night onward, for Takthan'Tor, they would no longer be an empty place filled with longing for a relationship of his own to rival the love between Moc'Tor and E'ranale.

When they entered, the room had been transformed. It was filled with scented flowers and decorative stones, and greenery hung from the overhead beams. A thicker sleeping mat than was usual had been added along with additional hides and throws. It was beautiful, and it warmed his heart.

Wry'Wry looked around and smiled. "What a special welcome. How kind of whoever it was to do this."

Takthan'Tor agreed and then swooped her into his arms and carried her over to the sleeping mat. "My prayers have been answered. My dreams have come back to life," he said as he gently set her down and eased himself next to her.

They had been apart for so long, living on memories of their time together. From now on, their memories would hold no tinge of regret or heartbreak.

Takthan'Tor gently raised Wry'Wry's face with his finger under her chin. How many times he had pictured this moment. He leaned forward and gently pressed his lips to hers. He inhaled her fragrance of pine and lavender, and her soft hair brushed his cheek. He slipped his arm around her waist and pulled her hard against himself. She let out a soft moan, and he kissed her closed eyelids, one after the other, then the tender spot just below her ear. He could feel her arms wrapped around the breadth of his back, urging him for more. He kissed her again. They had all night. They had waited so long. No need to rush it now.

Her hand was on his neck, and her lips on his became more urgent. Demanding. He throttled his desire to take her, wanting to make sure that her ardor was at its peak. He knew he would not be her first, but he wanted to make sure their first time together would live in her heart forever.

Harder, she kissed him harder and trailed her nails along his back, sending shivers up and down his flesh, raising all his hairs. Then she pressed his hips into her and said his name. Urged him to make them one.

Unable to resist, Takthan'Tor placed his manhood against her. She cupped her hand to guide him as he whispered in her ear how much he loved her.

Only he met resistance. *A maiden?*

"Wry'Wry," he said hoarsely, "are you still a maiden?"

"Yes," she said. "Kant and I never—"

"Oh, my sweet love," he said, and then he pressed forward into her, and she gasped out in pleasure and surprise.

Finally, they were one. The night was filled with the sound of their lovemating. Small gasps of delight, the crinkle of the sleeping mat under them, his muscular frame driving her into it again and again. Finally, he knew she had achieved release, and it was his turn. How soft she was, and yielding, giving under his thrusts yet holding him in a tight embrace at the same time until he exploded into her. It was glorious, more glorious than he could have imagined.

After their breathing calmed, he quietly got up and found her a soft hide to clean herself with. Then he lay back down, and after she was finished, pulled her over to cuddle up against him.

"I love you, Takthan," she said. "My first, last, and only love."

They spend the rest of the evening laughing together, caressing each other. More rounds of lovemating, some tender, some more passionate, and then they fell asleep intertwined together. As Takthan'Tor dozed off, he could imagine the spirits of Moc'Tor and E'ranale smiling down at them.

Wry'Wry was home. Not only back home but paired to the love of her life. She and Takthan'Tor spent a great deal of time over the next few days secluded in their own private world. As a kindness, Tensil had organized a slew of females to bring food to the Leader's Quarters to keep them from having to leave.

After a few days, Wry'Wry poked her head out into the hallway and looked around. "There is no one out here, come on!" she whispered.

Then she and Takthan'Tor sneaked out, and holding hands, slipped down the vacant corridor together. Wry'Wry giggled as they half-ran. It was very early in the morning, and they wanted to go for a walk all by themselves; it was fall, and the colors were at their most beautiful.

However, they ran into Tensil just coming back from somewhere.

"Oh! You have come out of seclusion," she laughed. She was holding a gourd of acorns.

Takthan'Tor looked at them. "We had the same thought."

"It was a wonderful seclusion. Do you know who decorated the Leader's Quarters?" Wry'Wry asked. "It was so beautifully done."

"Persica spent all day working on it with a group of our females, wanting to have it ready by the time of your pairing. It was also her idea for us to take care of your meals for a few days."

Wry'Wry shook her head. "What a gracious soul."

"Your parents are so happy; they told me so last night at evening meal," said Tensil. "Now, I will let you get on with your morning. And, Wry'Wry, when you get tired of Takthan'Tor, come and visit, and we will have another catch-up!"

Pan had returned to Lulnomia after a very long, healing, and rejuvenating time spent in the Aezaiteran Stream.

Rohm'Mok told her what had taken place with Lavke and how Irisa had helped Kyana, and she was devastated.

"I spent too long in the Aezaiteran Flow. I should have been here."

"I have no doubt the work you were doing with Wrollonan'Tor, and the amount of time you spent in the Aezaiteran Flow were equally important, if not more."

Pan set Tala down to play with her toys. "What he is teaching me—I cannot begin to explain how astounding his powers are. To think that I might someday be able to do what he does. There is so much no one knows about being a Guardian. It surpasses anything I could have imagined."

Rohm'Mok wanted to ask but didn't think he should.

"He is teaching me how to travel long distances by bending Etera."

"Bending Etera?"

"Well, not exactly. I cannot adequately explain it in words. But it is as if you could take the distance between two places and make their ends meet."

"I have no idea what you are talking about," Rohm'Mok chuckled.

"Picture the longest path leading away from Lulnomia down to the river. Now pretend it is made of hemp rope instead of rocks. Now take the two ends, one that starts at Lulnomia and the other that ends at the river, and bend them, so they touch. Now the distance between the two ends is not so far apart," she explained.

"It makes sense when you explain it that way. But how is that possible?"

"I have no idea," Pan laughed. "But it is. He showed me himself."

"You mean he took you somewhere far away?"

"He took me to Kthama," she said, her mood suddenly solemn. "It was wonderful to see the Akassa again. But it was also distressing. They are not thriving. In fact, they are floundering. They cannot let go of us, our presence in their lives, and they still see themselves as inferior, as less than us. In fact, two of the communities have sent members out to try and find us."

"They never will."

"No, they will not. But will some of them perish finding that out?"

"It takes time. They just need more time."

"I wish I believed that was true. But it is not just them. Their sense of inferiority is being handed down to their offling. And they, in turn, will hand it down to theirs. If something does not turn this around, who knows where it will end up. This is not the future of their making my father had hoped for. I am sure of that."

"Are you going to go back and talk to them?" he asked.

"No. That will only reinforce their belief that we are watching them and that we will have contact with them off and on."

"Does Wrollonan'Tor have a solution?"

"Yes. But it is a terrible one." Pan explained to her mate what she and Wrollonan'Tor had discussed.

When she was done, Rohm'Mok spoke. "You have to take this to the High Council. You must."

"Absolutely not," Hatos'Mok said. "How could you even consider it? What you are talking about is a crime against all of them. Unless you were going to ask for their permission?"

Pan knew it would be hard for some of the High Council members to understand, but she had not thought the Overseer would be one of them.

"There is no way to ask their permission, Over-seer. Surely you realize that. Besides, afterward, what difference would it make?"

"None, based on what you are talking about doing. But it might make a difference to your soul. You are talking about violating Sacred Law."

"Never Without Consent," she said.

"Exactly. I thought the goal was to learn from our mistakes, not repeat them?"

"It is not a mistake to right a wrong. If we do not do this, they will never move forward into the future of their making," she objected.

"They will create their own future; it just may not be what we think it should be. But who are we to say? Who are we to intervene?"

Pan could not help herself; filled with anger, she turned away, her jaws clenched. Then she whipped back around and asked, "*Who are we to intervene*? We have done nothing but intervene! Did we, the Mothoc, ask their permission when we created them? Did we ask their permission when we left them? All of them? So *now* it is our responsibility to ask permission to do what needs to be done—what we believe needs to be done?"

"But we do not all agree over what needs to be done," Hatos'Mok retorted. "Or shall I call a vote now on the merits of what you have presented?"

"Overseer—"

Hatos'Mok brushed her off and walked over to

stand directly in front of the rest of the High Council, effectively turning his back on Pan.

"Father—" Rohm'Mok moved forward to stop him.

"No. Stand aside. In this case, I am not your father, I am the Overseer of the High Council, and we *will* vote on this matter. How many of you support the idea of wiping out the Akassa's memories of the Age of Darkness, so no trace remains of our existence or anything that has gone before?"

Heads turned to one another. Hatos'Mok waited. One stood, then another. He waited some more. In the end, it was split with the slight majority against what Pan was proposing.

"The vote does not go your way, Pan. You are not to remove the Akassa's memory of the past or of our existence. Whatever happens now, it is up to them to find their way forward."

"This was not a fair vote," Rohm'Mok disagreed. "You did not let her present the entire argument before voting."

"They heard enough. Listen to me, I know that in the beginning, I did not support Pan as Overseer and Leader of Kthama, nor your relationship with her. But all that is in the past. I am not disagreeing with Pan personally. I am rejecting this idea of giving them a new past, a new history, no matter how positive she thinks the outcome would be."

"If the Akassa do not turn from this path," Pan argued, "if they do not build self-esteem in their offling, this self-degradation will only continue through the generations. Where will innovation come from? How will they enjoy their lives? What about their faith in the Great Spirit? How is that to survive this, what they perceive to be the loss of their Protectors? By refusing to help them, you are dooming them to a dark and hopeless existence."

"You do not know that is what will happen," Hatos'Mok retorted. "You can surmise that they are not happy, are even suffering, but you have no proof. I agree it is a reasonable assumption, but we cannot make decisions about this matter based on assumption."

Pan wanted to tell them all she was learning. She wanted to tell them about Wrollonan'Tor's existence, even to have him come and speak to the High Council members. She wanted to tell them how he had taken her to the High Rocks and that she had seen for herself their state of mind. But she could not. And so, she had lost her chance at winning the High Council over to what she knew was the only possible way of saving the Akassa.

"They call us their Protectors," she said, "and that is what we were to them. They feel abandoned, afraid, helpless. They don't believe they can rise above this. That is all I am talking about lifting from them. The sense of helplessness and despair. Why is that so wrong in your eyes?"

"I understand you feel a burden to right your father's wrongs—" said Tres'Sar.

"My father's wrongs?" Pan raised her voice. "My father's wrongs? You stood with him. I am staring right at you. You all took part in the division; you took part in the Ror'Eckrah. And yet now this is somehow violating their rights? You did not mind when you used the One Mind to deliver the Rah-hora. That was acceptable, but what I am proposing is not?"

"Let us concede the point that this is what the Akassa need. However, it would still be forced upon them Without Their Consent," Pnatl'Rar argued.

Bahr'Mok spoke up in Pan's defense. "As the Guardian said, we have done it before. What is the difference between what we did and what she is proposing?"

Hatos'Mok answered, "The difference is, we know better now. Yes, we did it before through the Ror'Eckrah. But we have learned since then. Making one mistake does not justify making the same one later."

"You believe that separating the Akassa and the Sassen was a mistake?" Rohm'Mok asked.

"No. Yes. Who knows? We do not know; that is the point!"

"That is exactly the point. We do not know," Pan said. "But it is the prerogative of leadership to make hard decisions, decisions based on the belief that what we are doing is the right thing to do. What would have happened if my father had not separated the Akassa and the Sassen? If he had not set in place the Rah-hora, which forbade contact between them? Would the Akassa not be wiped out in time, perhaps when the Sassen tired of life at Kayerm and turned a jealous eye back to the High Rocks?

"You forget," she continued. "You forget that what drove us to where we are now was the contagion that wiped out so many of our people, leaving so few males who were able to seed offling. Yes, those who could breed successfully still did, or we would not have the numbers we have now. But it was only by bringing in the Others' blood that the Mothoc blood continues to flow. If we had not done this, there would be no additional Mothoc blood of any strength. There would be only those of us who live now. And when we die off, when our blood no longer runs, Etera will die with us."

"What difference does any of this make? We are here now. What we do now is what matters," Hatos'Mok retorted. "And besides, the High Council has voted; there will be no interference. The Akassa must find their way on their own. We have meddled enough in their lives."

Pan started to speak, but the Overseer cut her off.

"No. I know you are the Guardian, but look what you have brought us to." He motioned around the room. "We are supposed to be united, and now we once again have division, this time within the High Council itself. I asked you to bring us unity, Guardian, not more division."

"Enough!" Rohm'Mok stood up once more. "How

dare you speak to Pan this way. She is the Guardian of Etera. Without her guidance, her blood, all is truly lost."

He stood in front of his father and shouted into his face, "Apologize. Now!"

Hatos'Mok stepped forward, chest to chest with his son, his face directly in Rohm'Mok's. "I will not apologize for doing what I think is right!" He stepped back and bellowed, "Now everyone out!"

"Half of the High Council was with you," Rohm'Mok said after closing the huge stone door of the private room they had found.

"Fewer than half," Pan said. "I expected more of them to understand."

"Perhaps in time, as they reflect on it, others will come around."

"Even if they all come around, I would still be violating the Sacred Law of Never Without Consent," Pan said.

"There is no rush to do this. Perhaps you can visit the High Rocks again in a year and see how they are doing then."

"I want to go home and hold Tala," Pan said. "Let us go home, please."

Ungut had stayed away but finally felt he needed to see his mate. The Healer, Pagara, had told him that Lavke had recovered and whatever had come over her was gone.

Joquel was sitting with her, and Lavke exclaimed when she saw him come in.

"Oh, please, please tell me you forgive me, that Pagara told you I am alright now." She reached out her hand to him.

Ungut was unsure of what to do. He still loved her, and he still felt that she and Joquel were his family. But he had not yet gotten over the shock that his mate had stolen Kyana's offling. With the offling being so young, it was a miracle that Joquel had found them in time. He had meant to ask his daughter how she had known where to look, but he would ask her later.

"Come in and sit with us," Joquel said to her father as she stood up.

Ungut frowned but did sit down as asked

"You do not have to say anything," Lavke said. "Just, please, give me a chance to prove to you that I am myself again."

"The Healer said that something came over you. So none of what you did was truly your responsibility?"

"Not all of it, but some of it was. I was jealous of Kyana being paired with Wosot. And I was unkind to her. And I did commit the crime of telling her family that Wosot had killed Nox'Tor to get him out of the way. That part is all true, and I am so sorry for that. They were horrible things to do. But the rest of it, stealing her offling—I do not know what came over me. I have done some terrible things, yes, but I would never have done that if I had been in my right mind. You must believe me."

Joquel came up behind her father and hugged him. He reached up and placed his hand on one of her arms.

"Let us try to begin anew and see how it goes," he suggested.

Behind him, Joquel let out a little cry of happiness.

"Oh, thank you," Lavke said with a huge sigh of relief. "I need to do something to try and make it right. Would you ask Kyana and Wosot to come and see me so I can apologize?"

"I will carry the message to them," he said.

Then Ungut turned to his daughter. "How did you know where your mother had taken Kyana's offling?

"It came to me all of a sudden. It was the place mother and I found together when we first came to Lulnomia. She said it was beautiful and that it reminded her of a place at the High Rocks where she used to take me after I was born."

Wosot and Kyana listened politely, and when Ungut was finished, Wosot spoke. "I appreciate the message, but I believe that for now, it is best if we do not have contact; we want only to raise our family in peace. Perhaps, in time, that will change."

"I will let her know," Ungut said.

When he had left, Kyana looked up at Wosot. "Thank you for that. I do not want to keep any animosity going; I just want to put it out of my mind for a while. But it sounds as if he has forgiven her; I do hope so."

CHAPTER 12

Kaisak's interest in Visha did not go unnoticed, and as Krac had predicted, Visha's mother, Kerga, was ecstatic at the possibility that the Adik'Tar might pair with her daughter.

Dak'Tor had mixed feelings. "If they are a good match, it will no doubt settle Kaisak down," he said to Iria. "If they are a bad match, eventually we will all pay."

"I agree. They are both somewhat high-strung. But maybe they will take their energy out on each other." It was the closest Iria would say that they both perhaps needed to be mated. Frequently.

"What of Moart'Tor?"

"He is your son; I know you have concerns, but I have no doubt Visha loves him, and no mother I know of would allow her offling to be dismissed. So if that is in Kaisak's nature, I doubt their pairing would happen."

"I hope this is not a trick to cause dissension between his followers and mine," said Dak'Tor. "I still have not decided what to think of him."

"That Moart'Tor is loved and protected is the most important thing. It will all hinge on Kaisak's intentions toward your son."

"Perhaps I should speak with him."

So it was that the next day, Dak'Tor sought out Kaisak.

"People are saying it is your intention to pair with Visha."

"So that is what all the muttering is about; the females stop talking when I walk by," Kaisak said. "And you are here to ask me if this is true?"

"Yes," Dak'Tor said.

"Are you objecting, if that is so? You have feelings for Visha?"

"Not necessarily objecting. And no, my feelings toward her are neutral."

"So it is your son's welfare you are worried about."

"Yes. There would be great benefits for Visha to be your mate, but where does that leave my son?"

"I am not Laborn. I would never harm an offling or threaten to harm one. What he did to your son Isan'Tor, placing him in harm's way with the coyotes, was unforgivable."

"And yet I understand you participated in it. You

were there while Iria was screaming and begging to go and protect our son. You restrained her while Laborn tortured her with fear."

"I was following Laborn's orders, and I have learned since then. Laborn was always angry, yes, but in the end, he became twisted, evil. I finally saw it. I am not him."

"Though you say you would never harm an offling, there is a difference between raising an offling as your own and simply tolerating him."

"I have told Visha that I would love Moart'Tor as if he were my own. There has been so much cross-breeding among our people that males are often not sure which offling really is theirs. And it is possible that sometimes the females do not know either. This is not an unusual situation."

Dak'Tor agreed; it was true. Until pairing was instituted, it was often uncertain who had seeded who.

"But," Kaisak continued, "that is why the work of Jamor and Lahru is so important. Now I can make pairing choices with a great chance of producing healthy offling."

Dak'Tor was surprised that Kaisak was talking to him as an equal. "Yes, that was a wise decision."

"I know there is bad blood between Visha and your mate. How does Iria feel about the possibility of my pairing with Visha?"

"She feels the same as I do; our concern is for

Moart'Tor's welfare. Will I have access to him? He is my son."

"If you want to be a part of his life, I have no intention of isolating him from you. Go home and tell Iria that if I pair with Visha, I promise I will raise him as my own, but that he will know you are the father of his bloodline. You need not worry about him; I give you my word as Adik'Tar."

Later, Dak'Tor told Iria about the conversation with Kaisak. "I believe him, yet I have a little hesitation. Perhaps his concern for Moart'Tor's welfare is that there is no mistaking he is a 'Tor. Perhaps he, like Laborn, fears my sister's return and her displeasure should she find that I or my offling have been mistreated."

"Do you want me to ask Useaves?"

"You trust her; I do not. But if you want to, go ahead."

"It will provide more information at least, even if we will not be certain how reliable it is."

Useaves answered Iria's question. "I believe Kaisak will do right by the offling. As for the match itself, I believe it will do them both good. They are both highly strung. One might see only conflict in that, but it also means that each will understand the other. It will also satisfy Visha's need to rise above you in the community."

"I had not thought that the source of our problems might be competition," Iria said.

"Visha is sensitive to public opinion. Being the mate of the Adik'Tar can only help soothe whatever wounds she is carrying that contribute to her being so— So touchy. I believe this will be good for everyone involved."

Having found out from Dak'Tor that the community was aware of his interest in Visha, Kaisak no longer tried to be subtle about it. He openly sought her out, whether just to say hello or to give her a present or a new toy he had made for her son. And each time Kaisak came to her publicly, she felt special. The one feeling she had longed for—struggled with for all her life—he was now freely bestowing on her.

Visha held out as long as she could, not wanting to appear too eager. But he was wearing her down, and she was enjoying the attention. She knew the other females were talking about her, and she knew they were not all in favor of the match as she had not treated them all well. But if she paired with Kaisak, she would at least be protected from whatever resentment they felt. As the mate of the Adik'Tar, no one would dare cross her.

Having made up her mind, she finally went to Kaisak, "I am ready to be paired to you if you still wish it."

Kaisak smiled. "Yes, I do. When?"

"Would you please announce it tonight? With the pairing perhaps in a few days?"

Kaisak's announcement was not a huge surprise. Visha's mother, Kerga, looked like the happiest person on Etera. The next few days were filled with excitement and there now seemed to be no one who did not think it was a good idea.

The pairing ceremony was quick. Kerga was keeping Moart'Tor for a few days so Kaisak and Visha could have some undistracted alone time. Though Kaisak had intended on waiting until Visha was ready, he mounted her that night. The release was intense. So much so that he took her three more times before daylight. When he woke, she was gone.

He tried to hide his panic. He realized in retrospect that he had been selfish. This was not a good start, and he chided himself for what he had done. He searched for her and felt a huge surge of relief when he found her outside at the fire.

She looked up as he approached, "I trust you slept well."

"I need to apologize."

"For what?"

"For last night."

"There is no need. It was what I expected. It was no different than it was with Dak'Tor. It is a physical release. I understand it." She went back to feeding the fire.

"I was selfish."

Visha looked up at him, "I am not a young female with dreams of being wooed. We are a good match. A partnership. It will work out."

Kaisak decided he would drop it but vowed to do better. He didn't want just a partnership. He wanted Visha to care for him, and he knew that in order to create that, he had to care for her first—and demonstrate it.

And from that day on, he committed himself to winning her heart. Everything he had told her was correct. He did want a true mate. He needed a confidant, someone he could trust. He had Useaves for counsel, but he did not completely trust her.

It was up to Kaisak to unite what was now his community, not Laborn's. Having no idea when the Promised One would be born, or if he had already been, he could not yet count on his plan to send Moart'Tor to Kthama to spy on the Akassa and the Mothoc. Moart'Tor was only a very young offling. He needed a united army far sooner—immediately, in fact—but even that would take time. Time, he worried, that he might not have.

Later, Kaisak made an announcement to Visha. "We are moving. I have selected a few locations. Please come and pick out the one which appeals to you the most."

Visha was finishing up feeding Moart'Tor. "Why

are we moving? I just moved in with you."

"I do not feel right, living in what was Laborn's space. You deserve a fresh setting. It was fine for Laborn, with Useaves and Gard just down the tunnels, but we need some privacy."

"How far away?"

"Not far. There is another collection of caves to the west of this system. I already scouted them out. It is only a short walk, but far enough away for us to create our own sanctuary from the commotion of the community."

Visha was not necessarily thrilled with being farther away from the main center of attention. She was enjoying her elevated status. But, in a way, it could be better. "I admit that it is hard never to think about Laborn having lived in this space."

Visha packed up Moart'Tor, and they set out on the walk to the new area. It was, as Kaisak had said, not that far, and in fact, it was a pleasant stroll. There were no briars along the way, nothing to snag her leg or body hair and pull tufts out.

"The opening looks east, which faces away from the direction of the weather. The morning sun will light up the entrance, making for cheery awakenings." He walked a few feet away and drew in the sand with his toes.

"We can set a fire pit here for when we wish to be alone for a while before retiring."

Visha looked overhead at the clear blue sky. She took it as a good sign and smiled at her mate.

Kaisak saw it. "Great! I will have Gard make sure there are no hazards, then ask some of the females to sweep it out and make sure there are no animal bones or other leavings in there. When they are finished, we can come back and inspect the different alcoves, and you can tell me which is your favorite. Then we will move our belongings in."

"Is there an area for Moart'Tor?" Visha asked.

"Of course. That was the first thing I looked for. Yes. One of the openings has another adjacent smaller cave. It would be a safe place for him to play when he is older, while you tend to your tasks. There is more than enough room for him to spread out his playthings. Best of all, he would not be able to get by you without your knowledge. Since we are the only ones going to be living here, you can pick a different cave for our sleeping quarters if you wish. It is all up to you, whatever you want."

"I must say that your thoughtfulness in this is a pleasant surprise."

"I am not a selfish male, Visha. I know our first night together got off on a wrong start. I was selfish then. But I was overtaken by your beauty, and I wanted you so much. I will make it up to you tonight, I promise."

Gard and the females completed their work, though it had taken a bit longer than Kaisak preferred. But he appreciated their thoroughness and went in to inspect the new area before going to get Visha. There was still enough daylight for them to get settled by twilight, which seemed right.

It took only a moment for his eyes to adjust as Kaisak surveyed the area. It really was very suitable. The ceilings were high enough that it did not feel too enclosed, yet not so high that their body heat would drift to the top in the coldest months and provide no benefit. And it was low enough that the coolness of the rock overhead would keep the temperature moderate in warmer weather.

Once their belongings were in place, food, and water storage, gourds, hanging herbs, dried meats, their sleeping mat, and Moart'Tor's covering and toys, it would feel like home.

"Everyone is talking about the new area Kaisak is moving Visha and your son to," said Iria.

"I think it is a wise move. Living where Laborn was, with all his anger and vindictiveness, and the memories of his terrible reign is not something I would want for you and our offling."

"I lived there more than long enough. It was a depressing place because his energy tainted the whole structure. Kaisak is wise to make a new start elsewhere."

"There are many of those smaller cave systems in

this area. A stroke of luck, really, for as the community grows, we will need to expand," Dak'Tor said.

"It is growing. And now that Kaisak has allowed some of the males to take mates, we will have even more offling running about. If only it could just be about what it is."

"If only it could be about living our lives and providing for our loved ones, you mean? Instead of building our numbers in order to annihilate the Akassa and Sassen."

"Do you think there is any chance he will change his mind about that?" Iria asked.

"We had a better chance with Laborn. I believe Laborn's bitterness warped his mind. I think when Shikrin was killed, it pushed him over the edge, so in a way, there was a chance that in time Laborn could have regained his sanity. But Kaisak is not insane. He is committed to what he believes is a sacred cause. It is not driven by avarice or resentment; it is, to him, well thought out and justifiable. We will have to bide our time, pretend to side with him, and hope that when it comes, we have enough strength on our side to thwart his plans."

Pan had returned to Wrollonan'Tor to tell him of her meeting with the High Council and that her proposal had been rejected.

He said little, only that they would, in time,

return to the High Rocks to see if the Akassa were winning their struggle for self-acceptance. He then refocused her on her training, working on increasing her connection to the Aezaitera without actually entering the stream.

"I did not know this was possible," Pan said.

"With much work and practice, it is. This is one of the many abilities I did not need to teach your father; he knew what he needed to do to achieve his life's work. But of you, much more will be required."

Wrollonan'Tor taught Pan how to reach down into the creative lifestream but maintain her own consciousness.

When she achieved the first level of this connection, she came out of it very excited. "I could still see you and Irisa somewhat, though as through a haze! But I was still me, only I was also aware of the peace and joy and bliss of the Aezaitera."

"It is through your connection to the Aezaitera that your powers will grow.

"The creative force of the Great Spirit is present in every aspect of Etera; even inanimate objects contain it. The life force, the Aezaitera, is only positive, but it encompasses both the male and receptive female traits. For example, the active, creative aspect allows us to access it to create the environment you see here that I live in.

"The receptive aspect means it is also subject to impressions in our realm. If negative, these impressions can distort the original positive life force once it has entered our realm. That is where the role of the Guardian is so important, as it is through us that the Aezaitera is cleansed of the distortion and returned to its original purity."

"There is only one power in creation, then."

"Yes. There is only one power, and it is positive, beneficent. But because the life force is impressionable, if negativity takes hold in this realm, it creates more negativity. Fear begets more fear. Belief in scarcity creates more scarcity as it drives others to take more than they need, to hoard, strengthening the very state they fear. Competition creates division. The entire cycle turns into a downward spiral. If this destructive aspect increases in strength enough to throw off the balance, and it overpowers the positive force, Etera itself could decay to where she would no longer support life."

"Are the Akassa contributing to this negativity?"

"Yes. By their fear, they are. But the greatest impact comes from the rebel Mothoc. It started with Norcab. His fearful and angry state affected others. They, in turn, spread their distortion to more and more of our kind. Because the Mothoc are so tied to the Aezaitera, their impact on the life force is far greater. And the negativity of the Akassa is increased by that of the rebel Mothoc. And its growth also feeds back into the vortex, and the two negative forces feed others and spread. All the vortices on Etera are connected like the rivers that connect and form the lakes, all ebbing and flowing into each other. The vortex below Kthama is the most powerful, so it has a greater effect on the others."

"When we left, we created a climate of fear in the Akassa."

"Essentially, yes. But it is being augmented and fed by the rebel Mothoc."

Then Wrollonan'Tor added, "The Akassa are suffering, and they are passing that suffering on to their offling, just as you told the High Council. But it is more than that, as you now understand. Unless it is stopped, unless something happens to remove that fear, it will only multiply, and the risk is that they will never come into their own. Their culture will flounder. They will never be who they were intended to be."

"And who they are intended to be is directly related to the coming of the Promised One?"

"Yes. But it is about more than freeing your father from the vortex, Pan," he said solemnly. "There is more to the Promised One's purpose than that."

"I understand. This is not just about saving my father. Or the Akassa."

"No. It is far more than that. It is about saving Etera herself."

Over the coming months, Pan's powers grew and grew. She learned how to command the Aezaitera, not to the extent Wrollonan'Tor could, but enough to create a small environment separate from his. She could traverse long distances as he did, which he had told her she needed to do to complete the assignments he would send her on. In between, she returned to Lulnomia to try to live a normal life with her family and the rest of the community.

But the day came when the Guardian of the Ages deemed Pan ready for her last and most important lesson, and so he called her back to him.

"You taught the Sassen Leader, Raddoc, how to bring about the Ror'Eckrah, the One Mind," Wrollonan'Tor said.

"Yes. I was impressed with how quickly he learned how to implement it."

"Good, as that will be as critical to the future as the Akassa's being freed from their fear and self-degradation. So, whoever initiates the Ror'Eckrah controls the minds of those who are joined in it. But not only that, the creator of the Ror'Eckrah has access to the creative power of the life force flowing in the blood of each linked body. Their strength becomes his strength, harnessing nearly limitless energy and creative force. And just as he controls their strength, he also controls their will, so they are entirely within his power. This is how your father enacted the Ror'Eckrah that delivered the Rah-hora to both the Sassen and the Akassa."

"Yes. But those joined must surrender willingly to the Ror'Eckrah," she said.

"No," Wrollonan'Tor said.

A chill ran like an icy sword straight through Pan. She felt as if the air around her shifted, and her feet were no longer on solid ground. "No," she said. "You are saying I can— You are asking me to—"

"You told Raddoc at Kayerm how powerful an army of joined Sassen would be. And how even more powerful would be a group of joined Mothoc."

"Those who joined with my father did so willingly," she stammered, her thoughts awhirl.

"Yes. But it was not necessary. Your powers have far surpassed what Moc'Tor's were even at the height of his abilities. You do not need their permission."

Pan sat down. "I need a moment," she said. He was asking her to form the Ror'Eckrah with every Mothoc, including the High Council members, against their will. Without Their Consent. To use them, their very own creative force, harnessed by hers, to remove the Akassa's memories. *Do I have the right? Do I have the strength?*

"No," she said. "I am not strong enough."

"Yes, you are. Because you would also have my power at your disposal."

"I could not overpower you!"

"No, you could not," he chuckled. "But you would not need to. I would augment your abilities. In fact, I would have to. Because even though your abilities are considerable, only I can provide the focus necessary to remove the Akassa's memory. It is not about removing their entire memory of the past because you will leave certain parts intact and instill some new ones. And we would not engage the rebel Mothoc."

"Because their negativity would also become part of it?"

"Yes. And it is their belief that the Mothoc still live among them which keeps them at bay, waiting to grow enough numbers before attempting to move against so many of their own kind. If they knew how vulnerable the Akassa are, they would attack them immediately."

Pan fell silent, as she often did when she felt overwhelmed and needed to collect herself.

"This is more than breaking the Sacred Law with the Akassa. Never Without Consent. This is breaking Sacred Law with my own kind," she finally said.

"Are you saying there are degrees of breaking Sacred Law?" he asked.

"I do not know. I do not know."

"You now understand what is being asked of you. But for now, you need to return home. Enter the Aezaiteran stream and rest afterward. Come back when you have made a decision and have peace in your spirit, one way or the other. But do not take too long, Pan. Each day, the Akassa's despair deepens."

CHAPTER 13

Pan did as Wrollonan'Tor said and entered the Aezaiteran Stream, but after that, she did not go home. She went to the Healer's Cove.

"How will I know what to do?" she asked aloud. "Tell me what to do. Mother, if you hear me, please help me. Please answer me!"

No answer came, except a memory of her experience in Wrollonan'Tor's world when she encountered the storm. She had pushed as hard as she could to keep moving forward, but when she could go no more, she stopped and waited it out. Should she continue to push forward, do as Wrollonan'Tor asked, or should she stop until she somehow knew what to do?

Though she was not in the salt cave where her powers were augmented, Pan decided to test her abilities. She set her intention to visit the High Rocks once more. It was not as clear to her as it had been when Wrollonan'Tor took her there; it was a little murky as if looking into shallows where the water had been stirred. But though she could not make out the people as clearly, the energy came through loud and clear. She then sent herself to the Far High Hills, then the Deep Valley, and then the Little River. When she was done, nothing could be more apparent. The Akassa were sinking, some communities faster than others, but they were all in trouble, and they did not have the ability to pull themselves out of the dark hole they had entered. Without intervention, the future that needed to take place would be lost.

Pan now realized that what she was called to do was more consequential than had ever been asked of anyone who had walked Etera before her. Her responsibility was first and foremost to the Great Spirit, and fulfilling that responsibility could very well cost her everything she loved most.

When she arrived back in Lulnomia, she went directly to her quarters. She waited, praying in silence until her mate showed up.

When he came in carrying Tala, she reached both arms out to him.

He set Tala down in her play area and came over to Pan. "What is wrong? Tell me."

"I am lost and do not know what to do," she sobbed as she fell into his arms. "I fear I am not strong enough for what is required of me."

"You are the strongest soul I have ever known. Whatever is required of you, I know you can do it. What are you so afraid of?"

"Of making a mistake. Of failing everyone I know and love. Of destroying the future of Etera—through either action or inaction." She raised her head to look at him, "And most of all, of losing everyone I love and care about. Of losing you and Tala."

"You cannot lose us. We are here, and we will always be here for you as long as we both live and breathe. What is this decision you are struggling to make that has you so distraught?"

"I do not struggle with the decision. I struggle with the cost. What if what I have to do means I might never see you or Tala again?"

Rohm'Mok had been so strong through everything. He had never faltered in his support for his mate and the responsibilities of her position as Guardian of Etera. He knew when he fell in love with her, when he paired with her, that the cost of loving her might be high. But it had never occurred to him that it might cost everything.

"What do you mean?"

"I know what I must do. And I know I must do it because it is the last thing I *can* do. I have not done everything that is within my power, and I cannot rest until I have. That was the wisdom given to me in the raging storm I had to face. I pushed on until I could not go another step. Then, and only then, did I stop."

Pan looked over at their daughter, playing

happily in her corner. "I am grateful that she was not born a Guardian. She has a chance at a normal life. A life spent on day-to-day issues, not tied up in meetings and burdened with tremendous obligations. To be able to put her own and her family's needs first, to grow old with those she loves and then join them someday in the Corridor."

"What are you saying? Will we not be together one day in the Corridor?"

Pan looked at him, her heart breaking. "Oh, my love. Yes. We will be together someday. But I fear that what I must do will cost me my time with you on Etera."

"What? How can that be? Why do you say that?"

"Promise me, if it happens that I must leave, that you will find another. That you will love again. And that she will be a mother to our daughter. Tala is young enough that she will not remember me clearly. There is no need for her to live with the heartache of losing her mother. Tell her of me, but nurture her love for one who can be a true mother to her. The one who will raise her and love her as her own. Promise me that."

"No! I will not promise you that because I cannot. There will never be anyone for me but you. How can you suggest that? Are you really saying you will leave us? Never see us again?"

"I may have no choice. Because in order to save it all, the thing that I must do will cost me everything I love." Pan sobbed openly in his arms now.

He rocked her, trying to soothe her, but his own heart was breaking. "Do not ask me to do this. Do not ask me to be this strong. I do not want to live without you. And you are Tala's mother. How can you leave her?"

"What am I to do? The future of Etera lies at stake. If I do not do this, everything will be destroyed. It will take thousands and thousands of years, but it will happen. Can I so selfishly choose my own happiness or my family's against the lives of all the generations to come?"

Pan could feel the battle raging within Rohm'Mok and his struggle not to cry out too. His wanting to support her, wanting to help her in her own pain, but drowning in his own.

Suddenly, he released her and stood up. "I need some time to myself."

As he walked through the door, he turned and said, "Do what you must do, and I will do what I must do. If it happens as you say it will, I will make sure that Tala is loved and cared for. But there will never be anyone but you in my heart; I can promise you that."

E'ranale turned to An'Kru. "My heart is breaking. Is there no other way?"

"She is strong; she can do this," he answered.

"But it is costing her every bit of happiness she has achieved."

"Even with everything we know of the love of the Great Spirit, of the tender care that guides our paths, it is still difficult to watch those we love struggle and suffer. But if nothing else, in time—*in time*—she will be reunited with her beloved and her daughter here in the Corridor. Never to be parted. And all the tears of her life in Etera's realm will be gone."

It was time. Pan and Wrollonan'Tor stood together. They began to chant the ancient sacred words. Words that created the vibrations designed to invoke the Ror'Eckrah, the One Mind. That which would unify the souls of the Mothoc and collectively call forth the creative power of the Great Spirit.

In the quiet sanctity of the night, every Mothoc soul within Lulnomia was drawn into a Connection. One more powerful than had ever been experienced by any of them, even those who had stood with Moc'-Tor. Their wills became Pan's. Their minds were locked into hers. They saw through her eyes, thought her thoughts, and the creative power that coursed through their veins was channeled into hers.

In the deep recess of each Akassa mind, a new history was created. One which did not include the Mothoc. There was no longer any knowledge of

Akassa or Sassen. From then on, they would be known to themselves only as the People.

Our People have lived for ages, formed by the hand of the Great Spirit out of the very dust of Etera. The Sacred Laws were given to us by the Ancients; the First Laws are immutable, but the Second Laws serve us, the People. These are the First Laws—" And Pan recited the First and Second Laws, lest any of the People forget them.

Gone was all knowledge of the Age of Darkness and of Kthama Minor. Knowledge of the Ancients, who were the Akassa's true ancestors, remained with only the Akassa Leaders. They alone knew that it was the Ancients who had betrayed the Brothers' trust and interbred Without Their Consent and that this period of shame, the Wrak-Wavara, was never to be spoken of openly. To the Leaders, the Ancients were to be known only as the Sarnonn. Finally, they knew that it fell to the People to make restitution. *To build a relationship with the Brothers, learn their language and customs, look out for them. This was their responsibility now.*

Through the power of the Ror'Eckrah, the massive creative force that she now harnessed, Pan touched the mind and heart of each and every Akassa. Before she broke the connection, she left them all with faith in the Great Spirit and the belief that they were enough. They were enough as they were.

Then, just as she had opened the Connection,

she released it. She opened her eyes and met Wrollo-nan'Tor's gaze.

"*Kah-Sol'Rin*," she said. "It is done."

The next morning, when the People awoke, they would discover a new world. A world filled with peace and confidence in themselves, in their own abilities. They would take comfort in the routines that made up their day-to-day lives. They would laugh with their offling and look forward to a future of living out their lives in service to the Great Spirit and to the Brothers.

The shame of the Age of Darkness was buried in the past, long gone. Only the Leaders would speak of it, and then only rarely, but the People's duty to the Brothers would be at the forefront of their minds. It would take time to win the Brothers' trust. But no matter how long it took, it was theirs to do, and they would not fail in their duty.

CHAPTER 14

When Pan returned to Lulnomia, they were waiting for her.

Hatos'Mok was standing at the head of the angry mob of High Council members.

Rohm'Mok was trapped behind them, trying to push to the front. "Pan!" he called out as he struggled to get through, but Hatos'Mok stepped forward, preventing him from reaching her.

"What have you done!" the Overseer bellowed.

"What I had to do. What was given to me to do."

"You have betrayed us all," he said.

"I have completed the work of my father. I have forever closed the Age of Darkness and freed the Akassa from the bleak future we abandoned them to."

"You have broken Sacred Law. Never Without Consent. Not only did you take the memories of the

Akassa, but you also invoked the Ror'Eckrah with us. Without *Our* Consent."

Pan had not expected any reaction other than this. Though some of the High Council members had stood with her when she proposed removing the memory of the Akassa, they would now no longer support her.

"Father!' Rohm'Mok shouted as he tried to reach his mate.

Hatos'Mok glared at his son. "No. You should be ashamed; there is no defending what your mate has done."

"Must we do this here?" asked Tres'Sar, looking around anxiously.

Hatos'Mok's eyes blazed at Pan, and he signaled for her and the High Council members to follow him. The crowd parted to make way as he led them to a private meeting room.

The heavy stone door creaked into place.

Hatos'Mok had lowered his voice, though he was still frowning harshly at the Guardian. "If you would like to try to defend your actions, please—go ahead. I would love to hear what your excuse is for the travesty you have just committed."

"If you do not already understand, nothing I can say will convince you," she replied.

Hatos'Mok was too angry to let it go that easily. "Oh, please, do try."

"I tried to have this discussion with you before,

and you cut me off. You said you were done listening. And now you are suddenly ready to listen?"

The other High Council members stood riveted to the debate.

"You have committed a grievous transgression. Not even the Guardian of Etera is above Sacred Law."

"To quote your last words to me on the subject, Overseer, *I will not apologize for doing what I think is right*."

"I followed your father. I supported him. I wanted to support you as strongly, but you have made it impossible. The only conceivable retribution for this is your banishment from Lulnomia."

Pan stood perfectly still. She had known it was coming, that it was the only possible outcome. She had violated Sacred Law, and as hers was the highest responsibility, so hers would be the gravest punishment.

"*No!*" Rohm'Mok cried out. "She has a family; we have a daughter. You cannot deprive Tala of her mother."

"Your mate should have thought of this before she took it upon herself to do what she did," Hatos'Mok snapped at his son. "She knew what the penalty would be. But I am not without compassion."

He turned back to Pan, "Guardian, undo the damage you have done. Form another Ror'Eckrah, restore the memories you have stolen, and all will be forgiven."

Pan slowly shook her head. "What I have done is

more important than whatever punishment you decree. This is bigger than you or me or anyone else. The needs of the community come before the needs of any individual."

"You quote Sacred Law after you have just violated it? Prepare yourself to leave Lulnomia forever. I will give you three days to say your goodbyes."

Rohm'Mok could not contain his anger any longer, and he slammed his fist down on a nearby table, splitting the rock slab in two. "She was only doing what she had to do!"

"Just as I am! The Guardian is now banished on my authority. Kah-Sol'Rin, it is done!"

Just then, the giant stone door was thrown open with a resounding crack. It shattered, and shards of rock flew everywhere.

Blocking the doorway was a behemoth covered in hair that was almost white. Whoever it was, the figure was larger than anyone had ever seen before and had to duck to enter the room. Following was the old female known as Irisa.

"Who—who are you?" Hatos'Mok managed to stammer.

"I am Wrollonan'Tor. Former Guardian of Etera." His voice was deep and confident and reverberated through the meeting room.

Every Mothoc there except Pan stood there aghast. There was silence while those in the room tried to make sense of what they were seeing and hearing. Rohm'Mok moved to Pan's side and put his arm around her waist.

"How can that be? Wrollonan'Tor died," Hatos'Mok said.

"A misunderstanding. I am who I say I am." Then the giant figure motioned toward Irisa as she stood behind him. "This is my daughter, whom you know as Irisa."

Hatos'Mok unconsciously placed both his hands on the side of his head as if trying to help his mind grasp what was happening.

"The Guardian Pan did what she had to do, and she did it with my help. You can ban her from Lulnomia, but you do so out of your ignorance and avarice."

"I bear her no ill will," Hatos'Mok said, dropping his hands and looking up at Wrollonan'Tor.

"Do you not? And yet your heart says you do." Wrollonan'Tor took a step forward, and everyone except Pan and Rohm'Mok quickly stepped back.

"You blame the Guardian for fulfilling her duty? She with the highest responsibility to the Great Spirit, to all of Etera? Do you not trust her commitment to doing what is best? What she did, she did for the good of all Etera and for everyone in this room and for your offling and theirs, for the Akassa and their generations to come, and the Sassen and theirs, too. If it were not for her courage, Etera would be doomed, and everything and everyone you love, and every creature that crawls on Etera's soil, or swims in the waters or flies through the air would perish.

"And for all this, you would invoke the harshest punishment you have at your disposal? Are you sure that taking from her all she loves is enough? Why not bind her and have her whipped with the Jhorrolax, her flesh bleeding and cut to ribbons in front of you? Will that satisfy you? Or is that too brutal even for you?"

Wrollonan'Tor took another step forward, and everyone backed up even further.

"It is my responsibility to fulfill the duties of my station. To administer justice." But Hatos'Mok's voice wavered.

"*As it is hers*. And that is what she did. She fulfilled her obligation as Etera's Guardian. She administered justice. To one extent or another, some of you were present to support Moc'Tor and his brother in interbreeding with the Others. Many of you participated in the first Ror'Eckrah. But Moc'Tor only took it as far as he could. It fell to his daughter, Pan, to finish it. And that is what she did.

"The Akassa were suffering through no fault of their own. They did not ask to be created—that was your doing. You agreed to it. They did not ask to be abandoned—that was your doing. You agreed to it. And when she stepped in and removed their suffering and gave them the possibility of a future free of the crushing anguish and despair that you abandoned them to, you turn on her, *the Guardian*, and accuse her of breaking the same Sacred Law you did."

Irisa stepped out and joined Pan and Rohm'Mok.

"So you, Overseer, have spoken," continued Wrollonan'Tor. "And with the authority granted to you by other Mothoc Leaders, you have banished her from Lulnomia. Pan will come and live with me, but not because of your decree. The mantle Pan bears is of the highest responsibility to the Great Spirit than of anyone who has come before. Etera's life itself rests on her shoulders. To succeed, she must abandon all personal gain. There is much I have to teach her, and she will be the greatest Guardian ever to walk Etera. And one day, she will return here, and you will greet her with open arms because the authority with which she will return to Lulnomia is far greater than that of your station. It will be with the same authority by which she did what she has done for the Akassa. The authority of the Great Spirit."

Heartbroken, Rohm'Mok spoke up. "Let us come with her. Me and Tala."

A softness came over Wrollonan'Tor's eyes as he looked at Rohm'Mok. "I am sorry."

Pan looked back at her mate with tears in her eyes. Then she turned to the Overseer. "I seek Bak'-tah-Awhidi, so my beloved may find another mate, and my daughter may be raised with a mother who is there to guide and love her every day of her life."

"Granted!"

"No. *I refuse it!*" cried out Rohm'Mok.

"You cannot refuse it, son. *Kah-Sol'Rin*. It is done."

"Now I am your son? A few moments ago, I was not. This cannot be happening." Rohm'Mok angrily paced away.

Pan went after him and took both his hands in hers. She looked deeply into his eyes. "I love you with the same sacred love shared by my father and mother. Ours is and will always be a legendary love. But my life is not my own, and you and Tala deserve a real life."

"I told you before, there will never be another. No matter what you say. So if the choice of Bak'tah-Awhidi is not up to me, then whether I ever let another into my heart is not up to you."

"Who will lead the High Rocks?" Norland suddenly asked.

"In time, the leadership of the High Rocks will fall to Pan's daughter. But for now, we will choose another," Hatos'Mok said.

"My sister, Vel," said Pan. "Dak-Tor is gone; she is next in line."

Hatos'Mok shook his head. "She is not prepared."

"Is anyone really prepared?" Pan asked. "She will learn. Rohm'Mok will be her counsel, as he has been mine." Pan was no longer trying to hide her tears from her beloved.

The Guardian of the Ages spoke, his voice booming through the room. "*Kah-Sol'Rin*. It is done."

Then he said to Pan, "Irisa will stay here with you at Lulnomia until you are ready."

And in front of everyone, Wrollonan'Tor shimmered out of sight, leaving behind him the shattered rock door.

Rohm'Mok pulled Pan into his arms. "Saraste'."

"We have a few days. Let us not waste them in saying goodbyes for which the time is not yet at hand."

"What now?" asked Pnatl'Rar.

"We must face the rest of the community. They are waiting for an explanation."

"What are we to tell them?"

Rohm'Mok was standing with his brother, Bahr'Mok, for support. "Why is that even a question? The truth. We must tell them the truth."

"What is the truth?"

"What is the truth? The truth is that my mate, Pan, the Guardian of Etera, fulfilled her responsibility—that which was given to her as a Guardian to do. And my father, the Overseer, banished her for it."

The air was spiked with emotion, and voices rose and fell.

Everyone was talking at once until Hatos'Mok yelled, "Silence!"

Just then, another figure entered the room. Heads turned to see the daughter of Wrollonan'Tor.

"This is a High Council meeting, Irisa," Hatos'Mok said. "You are not included."

"Well, I should be." And she continued to the front.

"With all due respect—" Hatos'Mok said.

"You think I do not belong here. Yet I have lived far longer than any of you can imagine. I have seen Leaders come and Leaders go. I have witnessed a multitude of triumphs as well as countless disasters. You think of me only as an old female who comes and goes between your communities. I know more about the lives of our people than all of you combined."

"Irisa is the daughter of Wrollonan'Tor," said Bahr'Mok. "She should join the High Council."

"So she can act as a spy for her father?" Hatos'Mok objected.

"You insult both my father and me," Irisa said. "I have no intention of spying on you, and neither is there any need. You underestimate the powers of a Guardian. My father already knows what takes place among you, and more importantly, what lives in each of your hearts.

"Fine." Hatos'Mok was still licking his wounds from the appearance of Wrollonan'Tor, and his chastisement. "What has taken place has the power to splinter our community. Everyone here experienced the Ror'Eckrah. There is no need to explain what happened; they are as aware as we are."

"Not everyone," said Irisa. "The offling were not

involved. So take care how you enter this into history. Take care not to cause them to lose faith in the Order of Functions lest you sentence them to the fate from which the Guardian has freed the Akassa."

"The daughter of Wrollonan'Tor is right," said Bahr'Mok. "We must not let our anger or confusion contaminate them. We must sit with this until we have sought the wisdom of the Great Spirit and made peace with it."

Hatos'Mok looked down to avoid eye contact with his son. He had acted rashly, out of anger and vindictiveness—just as Wrollonan'Tor had said. "In light of the recent events, I feel I must resign from my position of Overseer."

No one said anything.

"Because you have failed?" Irisa asked.

"Yes."

"As the Guardian herself said, no one is truly fully prepared for the challenges of leadership. Yes, you have made probably the worst mistakes anyone in your position could. But that is behind you now. You can only improve."

"Do not try to console me, Irisa," Hatos'Mok said.

"No one is angrier with my father than I am," put in Rohm'Mok. "But it is not wise to make crucial decisions when emotions are running this high. I suggest you think about this, unless the High Council wants to take a vote of no confidence?"

Not everyone agreed with Hatos'Mok's actions. He had acted rashly, out of anger, in using his authority to try to banish Pan. But they accepted Irisa's counsel and agreed to let him continue as Overseer.

The High Council members left the meeting room only to face a deluge of questions from a multitude of their people. The shock of the Ror'Eckrah and what had been done was like an open wound. They wanted answers, and they wanted them now.

"What happened to us? Did what we witnessed really take place?" The same questions were voiced over and over again. Hatos'Mok waited for some of the clamoring to quieten down before raising his hand.

"The Guardian used her abilities to create the Ror'Eckrah, the One Mind. In that state, she had collective access to the abilities of each one of us. It was her decision alone to remove the Akassa's memories of us, our time with them, and the Age of Darkness."

His statement was met with another uproar. Several of the other Leaders raised their hands and called for quiet, but it was several moments before everyone stopped talking.

"The Guardian believed that this was what was best for the Akassa," Bahr'Mok explained. "She said they were suffering, unable to get over our leaving them. They were weighed down by feelings of inferiority, feelings they were passing on to their offling. If she had not done as she did, she believed they were headed down a path into such a dark place that their culture would never recover."

Many voices called out. "Where is the Guardian?" "Where is Pan?" The Mothoc wanted to hear it from her.

Hatos'Mok raised his voice to be heard over theirs. "The Guardian is not available to answer your questions. She made the decision to form the Ror'Eckrah without the consent of the High Council. She acted in complete violation of First Law. She used all of us for her own selfish purposes. As a result of her actions, she has been banished from Lulnomia."

Somehow Hatos'Mok got the words out, but no sooner had he said them that the enormity of what he had done hit him hard. And it wasn't because of the melee that resulted; it was a deep conviction of what he had done.

He had banished the Guardian, the most revered and central figure of their culture. One whom every Mothoc through all of time had looked to for strength and guidance. The one among them who walked closest to the Great Spirit.

He had deprived his own people of the one whose presence was fundamental to their feelings of well-being and protection. Just as he and the High Council had inadvertently deprived the Akassa of their sense of well-being and protection by agreeing to leave them. Only, now, he had done the damage single-handedly.

Hatos'Mok had been worried about how the Guardian's action would divide Lulnomia, but that now paled in comparison to the act of Pan's banishment.

The last few days were the saddest of Pan and Rohm'Mok's lives. As great as had been their joy at finding each other, their anticipation of the lives they would share together, also as great was the heartache of knowing that this is where their paths diverged. That they would now go on to finish the rest of their lives apart.

It was their final day together, and they lay next to each other with Tala snuggled between them.

"I knew when I stood together with you at Ashwea Awhidi that there would be a price for loving you," said Rohm'Mok. "I knew the life as mate of the Guardian would ask much of me. I just did not know it would ask everything."

"I am so sorry. Had I known this was my destiny, I would never have paired with you," she cried.

Rohm'Mok placed a finger on Pan's lips. "Never say that. We have shared what few are blessed to know, and every relationship ends someday through the death of one of the beloved. To deny ourselves love because, in the end, the price will be our grief is to miss the greatest pleasure life can offer. To love and be loved in return."

"I do not know what my future holds," Pan said. "Wrollonan'Tor said that there is much more he has to teach me to prepare me for the coming of the Promised One. Live your life. Let Tala remember me if she does, but provide her with another mother. Please. And yourself with another mate."

Rohm'Mok was not going to continue to argue with Pan. But he knew in his heart there would never be another. And he would do his best not to wait, hoping for a stolen moment with her here or there. He would do his best, for that is all anyone can ever do.

The evening before she was to leave Lulnomia, Pan called everyone together to speak with them. She knew they felt hurt, betrayed, angry, and lost; she could feel it within her, so great that even she was unable to block it out.

As she entered, some pointed to her. Mothoc called her name, and many tried to reach out and touch her as she passed. She looked at each one of them and saw the devastation in their eyes. It took a while for her to make it through the crowd.

"There are no words to convey the sorrow that fills me in this moment, and I know also fills you. You all experienced the Ror'Eckrah, and no doubt you have been told of my reasoning, but I want you to hear it from me so there will be no misunderstanding."

Pan explained how the Akassa had been suffering, and how it was critical that their culture thrived and that they came into the future that was needed for the coming into being of the Wrak-Ayya, and eventually, the Wrak-Ashwea. She explained that what she had done was for all of Etera. That she knew she was born to this, just as strongly as her father had felt about what he did as Guardian. "It fell to me to complete the work of my father that the Age of Darkness might forever be closed, and the future could move forward as it should."

The crowd listened. Pan could feel the conflict within them. Some of them vehemently disagreed with what she had done but were torn by their respect for her position and recognition of the burden of her responsibilities. Others were devastated that she was leaving and would no longer walk among them. As heartbroken as she was at having to leave Lulnomia, she also knew that it was what had to be. And so she had to address their animosity, some of it nearing the level of hate, toward Hatos'Mok.

"You are aware that in punishment of my breaking Sacred Law Never Without Consent, both in binding you in Ror'Eckrah and removing the Akassa's memory, that I have been banished. I understand why the Overseer made this decision, and I will be leaving Lulnomia. But I am leaving because my duty requires me to do so, not because of the Overseer's decree. My actions did violate the Sacred law of Never WIthout Consent, but they were also in harmony with the Sacred Law that says the needs of the community overrule the needs of any one individual. In this case, I am the one individual. The Overseer banished me by his level of authority, but I leave to do what is required of me, no matter how much it costs me personally.

"Do not let this divide you. We have had enough of division. Make peace with what has happened, or your anger and negativity will contaminate the vortex far more quickly and more deeply than could the rebels. I have freed us all from the shadow of the Age of Darkness, so do not let my sacrifice be in vain. Become again the united community of Mothoc that we once were. Trust the Order of Functions. Honor my sister, Vel, as the new Leader of the High Rocks."

Then Pan called her sister to the front and solemnly handed her the 'Tor Leader's staff. The mantle of leadership of Kthama's community had passed to Vel. Pan saw the grief in her sister's eyes, and it was another knife in her heart.

Every pair of eyes was locked on the Guardian.

"Leaving here will be one of the hardest things I have ever done. Not only am I leaving all of you, but I am leaving my beloved mate and daughter. Please look after them. The Overseer has granted Bak'tah-Awhidi—"

She had to stop as the crowd broke out in an uproar.

"I love Rohm'Mok with all my heart." She looked over to him and the tears she had been stalwartly holding back finally rolled down her face. "My fervent prayer is that he will find another to walk with through the years and to be a mother to our daughter. Had there been another way, I would have taken it. Gladly."

That was the unanswered question that would haunt each soul in the dark hours of the night. "What would *you* be willing to sacrifice to save it all?"

It was time. All the Mothoc had been asked to stay in their quarters to allow Pan to leave Lulnomia in privacy. The halls, the Great Entrance, all of the community areas were empty. It was as if she was the last occupant. Or the first. Or the only.

As for Rohm'Mok, Pan had asked him to leave this for her to do alone. Standing in their quarters, she took one last look around. The 'Tor Leader's Staff, which had been stored high enough to be out of Tala's reach, was no longer there, but she longed to touch it once more. To run her hand down the bark, worn by so many hands before hers. To feel the heft of it in her hand one more time.

Her thoughts went to her brother, Dak'Tor, who held the sacred crystal in his possession. What was his life like? Had he found any peace at all? Would she ever see him again? Then she went to her personal table and picked up the red jasper stone Rohm'Mok had given her. The one Ravu'Bahl had dropped in front of him in the snow. She wanted to take it with her, but she remembered how happy she was when she had removed Lor'Onida's scroll, and her mother's red jasper stone had fallen out. She had grieved its loss and then celebrated its return. Perhaps this would come to mean something to Tala when she was old enough to understand that it had belonged to her mother.

Pan walked slowly through the empty halls of Lulnomia toward the Great Entrance. Memories of leaving Kthama flooded her. Now Lulnomia had come to mean to her what Kthama had once meant. More goodbyes. More loss. And yet the promise of happier days to come. Someday. Always someday.

One last breath, one last sigh, then Pan stepped outside and turned her face toward the life that lay before her.

Wrollonan'Tor was waiting.

EPILOGUE

Though she knew there would be no more communication between them until the Chief decided it, Sitka still visited the great oak tree. Her fear had subsided, and now she felt only sadness. She wished she had been stronger, had been able to accept what had been shared with her about the origin of Tensil's people. Perhaps if she had not reacted so badly, it would have turned out differently.

She and Tocho did not speak about what had happened, though both wanted to, so the Chief's admonishment held. Tiva was still disappointed that they were no longer making contact, so Tocho started making up stories for her about Oh'Mah. She knew they were just stories, but she enjoyed them, and it lifted her sorrow and satisfied her curiosity enough.

One night, after a particularly exciting story, Tiva

asked her brother, "Do you think you will ever see them again?"

Tocho did not know how to answer, as she still did not know that the people who had saved him were not Oh'Mah. They were two different tribes.

"Only the Great Spirit knows that. Now get some sleep."

Sitka had never recovered from the loss of her true love, killed at a young age. She never had her own children, but she loved all those in the village, and they and their children loved her in return. Later, when Tocho and Tiva grew up and had families of their own, their children spent a great deal of time with the Medicine Woman.

Sitka lived to a very old age, and when she was finally dying, she asked to be taken to the great oak tree, which was still standing as tall and strong as ever. She was hoping that she might see Tensil or one of the others one last time. But no one came. Tocho found Tiva's red jasper, placed right in the center of the circle they had used to communicate. He pressed it into Sitka's hand, and she smiled for a long time, believing that somehow Tensil had known she was dying and had left it there for her as a symbol of their bond.

After she passed, Tocho returned the stone to

Tiva, to whom it had originally belonged, as Sitka had asked.

It took generations for the People to establish a relationship with the Brothers. In time they developed a shared language, a modification required by the Brothers' different vocal structure, and one that changed the People's language from the original Mothoc. The People adopted some of their ways, and the language intermingled. Some of the People took names for their offspring from the Brothers' culture.

Much of the Mothoc culture was forgotten.

The story of the Wrak-Wavara, the Age of Darkness, and the betrayal of the Brothers was passed only from one Chief to the next, and Medicine Woman to Medicine Woman. It was a time of deep disgrace with the details of how it was accomplished never revealed to any of the Brothers.

The Brothers had no knowledge that the Mothoc and the Sarnonn were not the same. It would be thousands of years until they would learn the truth.

Unlike the Akassa, the Sassen had continued undisturbed in their lives without the Mothoc. Of the two groups, the Sassen had fared the best, perhaps because they were much like the Mothoc. They saw aspects of the Mothoc in themselves, and of course, in their culture. They had missed their friends and family, but they did not suffer the despair that had befallen the Akassa.

For the most part, the Mothoc culture lived on in the Sassen, though eventually, the old ways of mating returned with the restriction of one male to one female abandoned. It was a shift that would take its toll in time, bringing them back to the inbreeding situation that had caused the Ancients to interbreed with the Brothers in the first place. The message of the Rah-hora that they would be destroyed if they made contact with the Akassa, though misinterpreted, was effective, and they now diligently kept away from the People.

The Sassen rarely revealed themselves to the Brothers. In time the Brothers came to believe that perhaps they had left and no longer lived among them. The Brothers, never having seen a Mothoc and a Sassen side by side had no idea there was more than one Sasquatch that had lived among them.

For thousands of years before the time of Moc'Tor, the Mothoc had lived in peace and harmony, honoring the Great Spirit and fulfilling their duty to Etera. But change is the nature of life, and it fell to Pan's father, Moc'Tor, to lead his people down a path of division. A division necessary to avoid the eventual loss of the Mothoc blood from Etera. And without the blood of the Ancients, Etera would sicken, falter, and die. And so the Age of Darkness fell. The Wrak-Wavara.

Pan, Moc'Tor's daughter, was destined to be the last of the Mothoc Guardians. Like her father before her, she had pledged her life to fulfilling her duty as Etera's Guardian. By her hand, by her sacrifice, she finished the work of her father.

The truth of the Age of Darkness had been sealed away, its secrets buried behind the massive stone concealing what had been the entrance to Kthama Minor. The bodies of Moc'Tor, E'ranale, and Straf'Tor were waiting in the tomb of the Chamber of the Ancients, perhaps never to be discovered.

And lastly, the final measure. All memory of the Mothoc and the Sassen, of their very origin, erased from the memory of the Akassa, the People.

Though it had cost everything she loved, Pan had set Etera on the only path that could lead to her salvation.

For thousands of years following, the Sassen and the People would come to know that same peace and harmony that the Ancients had once enjoyed. Until the time of Khon'Tor, descendent of Moc'Tor and Takthan'Tor.

In his lifetime, Khon'Tor would see both the fall of the Age of Shadows and the birth of the Promised One. And eventually—

Ah, but that is a story for another time.

INTERVIEWS WITH THE CHARACTERS

Rohm'Mok: Leigh. I am not happy with you right now. I only came because Pan pleaded with me.

LR: You are upset because Pan has left Lulnomia. I understand.

Rohm'Mok: How could you do this to us? To Pan, to Tala? There have been so many challenges in each of these books for many of us.

LR: Life is full of ups and downs, Rohm'Mok, even in Lulnomia. And this is the Age of Darkness, a tumultuous time of growth and evolution for all. But let me ease some of your pain. You will live to see Pan again. I promise.

Rohm'Mok: And Tala? What of her?

LR: Yes, she will see her mother again. And to you, it will not seem that long a time that you are apart, I promise. Because just as time passes differently in the Corridor, so it also passes differently in the books.

Wosot: I am grateful that Lavke has recovered and our offling is safe. I hope she does not cause any further trouble.

LR: Her causing you trouble is over. Irisa has healed her through the power of the Great Spirit given to her.

Tocho: What about my sister and me? And Sitka? Will we be back in another story?

LR: I am pretty sure you will, perhaps in a short story or two!

Takthan'Tor and Wry'Wry walked in.

Takthan'Tor: I cannot thank you enough for our happy ending. I was committed to making the best of it with Persica, and she would have been a good mate to me and I to her. But my heart will always belong to Wry'Wry.

Wry'Wry: Yes, thank you, Leigh. And Persica, what a true and wonderful friend. I hope she finds happiness.

LR: She does. I guarantee it.

Wry'Wry: Where are all the others? Only a handful of us is here. I see none of the High Council members; none of them have come.

LR: It is up to each of you whether you want to talk to me at the end of the story. I respect your preferences. Some of you are more private than others.

Rohm'Mok: My father did not look good at the end. I can understand why he did not come.

Norland: What about the Sassen? There was virtually nothing about them in this book.

LR: They have not struggled as the People have. Their existence pretty much goes on, undisturbed, until Series One.

Norland: Excuse me, Leigh, but do you know you wrote these series backward?

LR: Oh, Norland, forgive me for laughing. Yes, I do. My hope is that readers of this series, if they have not read Series One, will still do so. They are intertwined, after all. They were not really written back-ward, but if you think of them chronologically, then I understand they would seem that way. It is just a more interesting way of presenting the story.

Kyana: What happens to us now?

LR: Enjoy your lives. If I need you again, you will know. I will see some of you in Series Three. Others of you, no, but you will live on in the hearts and minds of our readers. And in mine.

Rohm'Mok: What about Pan's brother, Dak'Tor. Will she ever see him again?

LR: Her brother still has a long road ahead of him. As hard as it has been, his life with the rebels was exactly what he needed. He is no longer the Dak'Tor who betrayed Pan. It will all work out in Series Three. Until then, enjoy your imaginary lives until we meet again.

Wosot: I did not know that we could do that. This is wonderful. Who makes up these rules?

LR: Well, since it is coming from my imagina-tion, I guess *my world—my rules* applies! And I have just decided that you live on between my stories.

Kyana: That is great news.

LR: Think of it as a Broadway production. Oh dear, that doesn't mean anything to you. I was going to say, if you think of these stories as plays, then when the play is over, the actors still go on elsewhere until the next production.

Norland: We are happy and cannot wait to see

where the story goes when you next summon some of us.

LR: Well, it isn't like a seance, but I understand. Be on your way now. Blessings.

Takthan'Tor: I have no idea what you are talking about— Broadway— Seance— But it does not matter. Until we see you again, be well.

PLEASE READ

So, you made it through all five books of Series Two. You may, like me, be a little sad to come to this point, which I am pretty confident is the end of this series. If you have not read Series One and jumped into Series Two with both feet, I encourage you still to read it. Series One, Wrak-Ayya: The Age of Shadows, covers the journey of the People thousands of years following what takes place in this series. There also are some elements from Series One that are fleshed out in Series Two. Especially if you are going to continue onto Series Three Wrak-Ashwea: The Age of Light, which picks up where the storyline was left at the end of Series One. The same characters from Series One (Khon'Tor, Adia, Acaraho, etc.) will flow through to Series Three, as well as some of the characters from Series Two (if you did not pick up this fact, the Mothoc live thousands and thousands of years).

In Series Three, the People stand at the dawning of a new era. But the rebels, having grown in number and strength, pose a serious threat to all of Etera—their negativity poisoning the very creative life force, the lifeblood of Etera. The rebels' influence, coupled with the negativity of the Waschini, must be stopped.

In this book, I touch on the concept of staying in the present moment. If you are even slightly interested in this subject, I highly encourage you to engage with the works of Eckhart Tolle. He is a contemporary spiritual teacher who teaches the power of living a life of presence. These are powerful works that have personally helped me. You can also find his offerings on YouTube. His website is https://eckharttolle.com/

Lastly, how to stay engaged with me:

Follow me on Amazon on my author page at https://www.amazon.com/Leigh-Roberts/e/B07YLWG6YT

Or you can subscribe to my newsletter at: https://www.subscribepage.com/theeterachroniclessubscribe

I also have a private Facebook group at The Etera Chronicles

If you enjoyed this book, please leave a positive review or at least a positive rating. Of course, five stars are the best. If you found fault with it, please email me directly and tell me your viewpoint; I do want to know. But a negative rating truly hurts an author. You can return to your Digital Orders and find the book there, and click on Write a Product Review. Or, you can find the link to leave a product review on the book link on Amazon, where you purchased or downloaded the book.

Positive reviews on Goodreads are also greatly appreciated, as important as those on Amazon, really.

Thank you again for your faithfulness!
Blessings.
Leigh

ACKNOWLEDGMENTS

The One-Who-Is-Three, whose love inspired me to write this story of faith and self-discovery along the path leading us Home.

Made in the USA
Las Vegas, NV
20 February 2024